MURDER SO PRETTY

Eagle Cove Mysteries #3

NORA CHASE
ANNE CHASE

Thomas Publishing

ISBN-13: 978-1-945320-07-1

For John and Cathy Hindmarsh

CHAPTER 1

Ah, the joys of spring. The cheerful rays of the warming sun. The bright scent of hope wafting happily through the air. Nature in all its variety bursting anew from every nook and cranny — eager, beautiful, vibrant, and determined.

One doesn't expect murder in this most optimistic of seasons.

At least I didn't.

Though I should have. If you're aware of my recent past, of my autumn and winter fighting off desperate killers and violent death, then you'll understand why I look back at Eagle Cove's disaster-filled spring with regret and more than a twinge of guilt. Had I been just a bit more attentive, perhaps I could have anticipated — even prevented — the murderous mayhem soon to engulf our small New England town.

Alas, in the crucial moments before chaos came calling, I noticed exactly nothing — nada, zippo, diddly-squat — because I was focused entirely on something else: Doing all I could to ensure that the opening reception of the Eagle Cove Flower Show got off to a smooth and problem-free start.

The annual flower show, a four-day festival of all things floral that draws tourists by the thousands, is a big deal for our little town. In something of a coup, my cafe had been hired to cater the opening reception, an opportunity I was determined to not mess up.

On the afternoon in question, under a big white tent on the grassy green lawn of the Eagle Cove Common, I was anxiously scanning the reception for tasks to tackle and issues to avert, blissfully unaware of our town's imminent rendezvous with calamity. Around me, a hundred invited guests — judges, organizers, donors, the media — were gabbing away merrily, dressed in their spring best. The mood was festive. Laughter and conversation filled the air.

Across the tent I spied Janie McKendrick, my cafe co-owner, setting a tray of cucumber sandwiches on an appetizer table. Waiters in tuxedos, hired by us for the occasion and looking spiffy and crisp, circulated with bottles of wine and pitchers of fresh-brewed iced tea.

I watched with a smile as Janie's scrumptious

offerings — crustless sandwiches, delicious pastries, and freshly baked scones inspired by the traditions of English afternoon tea — got snapped up by the hungry crowd. Janie had worked incredibly hard on the menu and it was gratifying to see the attendees enjoying what she'd prepared.

Throughout the tent, gorgeous flower displays — exuberant explosions of roses and peonies, daffodils and tulips, orchids and lilies and so many other beauties — were positioned on pedestals for guests to admire from every angle.

After months of careful planning and a busy night and morning setting up, the reception seemed to be going smoothly, at least so far.

A rumble from my stomach reminded me that I'd neglected to eat anything since hurriedly scarfing down one of Janie's cranberry scones at dawn. I was thirsty, too, the glass of iced tea I'd guzzled a short while earlier barely denting my thirst.

I was eyeing the appetizer table hungrily, wondering if I could sneak in a quick bite, when I heard my name and turned to find Doris Johnson, Eagle Cove's mayor, weaving toward me through the crowd. A tall woman in her late fifties, with short-cropped gray hair and smooth ebony skin that didn't show her age, the mayor was dressed for the reception in a lovely pale blue skirt and a festive blue-and-yellow flowered hat.

"Sarah," she said, her voice brimming with affection. "You and Janie have done a wonderful job with the reception."

"Thank you," I replied, pleased to receive the mayor's approval.

"Have I ever told you how grateful we are that you moved back to Eagle Cove and reopened your aunt's cafe?"

"You have, yes," I said, noting her effusiveness. Mayor Johnson was great at her job and relentless in promoting Eagle Cove's interests, but her demeanor was typically more measured and firm, like a polite bulldozer.

"Well, I haven't said it enough." To my surprise, she pulled me in for a hug. "I think you are the best!"

"Thank you," I managed to reply as she squeezed. Public displays of affection weren't part of the mayor's usual arsenal. Perhaps I was experiencing a new side of her?

"And I want you to know, I accept you for who you are."

My brow furrowed. "Accept me for...?"

"Oh, your nosy nature gets me so worried sometimes," she said with a laugh, her grip intensifying. "But then I remember you can't help it and I tell myself, 'Doris, you just gotta deal. Girl can't change who she is.'"

With the hug showing no signs of ending, I

began plotting my escape.

"Of course, you make me so mad sometimes," the mayor continued happily. "Always finding dead bodies and tangling with killers and diving into trouble. Oh, you definitely keep me on my toes."

"Well, it's not that I intend —"

"It's who you are. I have to accept that. Sarah Boone, meddling murder magnet. My worst nightmare!"

Then she laughed again.

With difficulty, I managed to extricate myself.

"Mayor, I don't think I —"

"Now don't be getting upset with me for delivering a dose of truth. Everyone loves you. Reopening the cafe was a wonderful thing."

Maybe it was the humidity, I speculated. Or the warmth of the lovely spring day. "Listen, can I get you a glass of water? It might good for you to —"

"And you know, when I say *everyone*," the mayor said, playfully arching an eyebrow, "I really mean that fine-looking sheriff of yours."

"Mayor Johnson," I said, slightly shocked.

"Mmm hmm. Fine indeed, and wrapped around your little finger. Good for you, girl."

Before I could respond, the mayor swayed slightly. "I need some air."

"Let me help you."

"No, I'm good." With a final warm smile, she

pivoted and threaded her way through the crowded tent, stumbling only slightly.

I tracked her progress and breathed a sigh of relief when she made it outside without incident. Perhaps she was a bit dehydrated? A glass of wine too many?

I glanced around the gathering, torn between following to make sure she was okay and staying put to keep an eye on things. The event appeared to be going wonderfully, the crowd in a jovial mood, the din of conversation in the tent deafening. The laughter rising above the hubbub was music to my ears.

Across the tent I spied Donald Benson, one of my downstairs neighbors, laughing uproariously at something Janie had just said.

Janie, in turn, was looking at him with a confused expression.

Which seemed *odd*. Mr. Benson, cautious and reserved by nature, wasn't the type to get uproarious. And cracking jokes wasn't Janie's thing. So why was —

A nearby explosion of laughter startled me and I whirled to find Gabby McBride, my other downstairs neighbor, guffawing hysterically with her gang of fellow octogenarians, Mrs. Chan, Mrs. Bunch and Ms. Hollingsworth. Gabby's friends were visions of spring in their lovely yellow, pink, and soft blue dresses, while Gabby's neon pink and fluorescent purple muumuu seemed especially bright and cheerful.

"Girls," Gabby was practically screaming, bent over with laughter. "You're killing me!"

Everyone, it seemed, was having a terrific time — a *really* terrific time. Maybe the mood was upbeat because folks were relieved to be outside enjoying the fine spring weather after a long and brutal winter?

Yes, the weather explained it, I told myself. Sunshine and fresh air were wonderful mood enhancers.

At the far end of the tent at the judges' table, I noticed our head judge, the eminent horticulturist Beauregard Greeley, dozing in his chair, head bent down.

With his white hair, pink skin, pale blue flannel suit, yellow bow tie, and roly-poly build, he looked like an Easter egg.

I found myself giggling. Why hadn't I realized that before?

Across the tent, Mr. Benson was swaying slightly. Then to my surprise he began performing what seemed to be....

A hula dance?

The crowd gathered around, cheering him on.

He looked so silly!

And yet....

I felt it then — a wave of lightness rolling

through me. My spirits soared. Everything became brighter and peppier. The colors of the flowers on the tables intensified. I gasped with astonishment.

A big grin appeared on my face and wouldn't go away, no matter how much I tried to get rid of it.

But why get rid of it? It was such a lovely day!

Everything was delightful!

Even poor Professor Greeley, he of the nasty temperament, he of the snooty snottiness and snotty snootiness, he of the over-the-top rudeness and overbearing meanness, he who had so viciously insulted Janie's delicious scones, he who effortlessly brought my blood to a boil every single time he opened his nasty mean awful mouth — even he seemed quietly charming now.

The poor thing was misunderstood, that was all. Beneath that egg-shaped exterior beat a lonely heart yearning — aching — for the joy of human connection.

I couldn't let him miss out on the fun. How wrong would it be to let him sleep through this most effervescent of days?

"Professor Greeley," I called out. "Hey ho, you cute little thing."

I bustled over. The poor little egg-man was sound asleep.

"Professor," I said cheerfully. "Time to wake up."

I reached out and gave his shoulder a gentle shake.

His head rolled back.

Which seemed *odd*.

I bent closer.

The professor's eyes were wide open —

Staring at me without seeing —

And filled with *blood*.

I let out a gasp.

The poor little egg-man was dead!

CHAPTER 2

The plot to murder Professor Beauregard Greeley began two days earlier.

At least in my mind.

At least — and I understand the importance of being precise about this, given what occurred — that's when the enormously satisfying *fantasy* of Professor Greeley flying forever from this mortal coil first flashed through my fevered consciousness.

I suppose I should feel guilty about wishing such a dire fate upon a fellow human being. My homicidal musings seem, well, *unseemly* now.

Or maybe I should cut myself some slack and accept that, when it comes to Professor Greeley, the emotion I will always feel most is annoyance — with myself — for letting that awful man slip past my defenses and under my skin.

I met him two days before he died, on an

otherwise cheerful morning inside Emily's Eats, the cafe that Janie and I run in downtown Eagle Cove. It's a friendly place, our cafe, situated on the ground floor of a three-story building on Main Street, with tables and chairs near the front windows and a row of red booths along the wall parallel to the long display counter. Since opening our doors in January, we've attracted a loyal clientele thanks to Janie's wizardry with scones, muffins, croissants, and more. With the summer tourist season drawing near, the two of us were actively planning an expansion of the menu to include hot breakfasts and limited lunch offerings.

As was usual in the mornings, Janie was in the kitchen whipping up yet another batch of her signature scones and I was at the cash register in front, doing my best to keep pace with the hustle and bustle of the morning rush.

The cafe's regulars were there in force. Mr. Benson, a dapper fellow in his seventies who lived in one of the apartments above the cafe, was perched on his favorite stool at the counter with his morning coffee and blueberry muffin, carefully perusing the latest edition of the *Eagle Cove Gazette*. Along with his usual tweed jacket, he wore a red bow tie that added a dash of color to his otherwise reserved appearance.

I pointed to his sleeve. "A crumb," I whispered.

He glanced down, removed the offending morsel, then set it on his plate. "Thank you, Sarah."

At her preferred table by the front window, our resident psychic, Hialeah Truegood, was sipping Earl Grey tea as she awaited her first client of the day. With her vivid tumble of red hair and her fondness for dramatic full-length silk gowns, Hialeah came across as larger-than-life. But in the six months since her arrival in Eagle Cove, I'd come to realize she was actually on the quiet side, her manner diffident, her voice soft, her Southern accent lovely and soothing. An observer rather than an instigator by nature, she inserted herself into situations only when required by her visions.

As for those visions…. I freely admit a gut-level skepticism when it comes to psychics and their so-called powers. But I couldn't deny Hialeah's uncanny knack for knowing about things before they happened. More than once, her predictions had ended up being spot-on, bang-on, dead-on right.

Catching my eye, she waved me over. After a quick glance around to confirm that everyone was settled in with their coffees and treats, I went to her table.

"Sarah," she said, her voice soft and low. "The spirits want me to share a message."

Hialeah did this sometimes — pulled me aside to offer tidbits from her non-corporeal pals. Usually the news was good, but on a couple of occasions, the stuff she'd shared had been downright ominous.

I girded myself for the latter. "Oh, is that so?"

"The spirits say what's coming is not your fault."

A frisson of alarm shot through me. "What's not my fault? What's coming?"

She glanced around to make sure no one could overhear. "They won't say. But they insist it's important — crucial — for you to remember two things when the time comes."

I have to confess: Hialeah's spirit connections both worried and intrigued me. "I want to be sure I have this right. There are two things I need to remember 'when the time comes.' What does 'when the time comes' mean?"

She shook her head, vexed. "They're being quite vague, I'm afraid. But they keep repeating two phrases over and over."

"Go on."

"The first phrase is, 'The stain reveals.'"

I frowned. *What the…?*

"And the second is, 'All must bear witness to the trap.'"

I wasn't sure how to respond. It sounded like nonsense. "That's it? 'The stain reveals?' 'All must bear witness to the trap?' Those are the phrases?"

"I don't understand them either."

"Does this happen a lot? The spirits say something cryptic and you're like, um, *what?*"

She shrugged apologetically. "As a general rule, I share only what is clear. But the spirits insisted."

"Thanks, I guess? If your spirit friends say something more...."

"I'll let you know right away."

As I returned to the register, I heard my name and turned to find Gabby glaring at me impatiently. As usual, she and her crew — Mrs. Chan, Mrs. Bunch, and Ms. Hollingsworth — were holding court from the red booth nearest the door, strategically positioned to receive and dispense the gossip that Eagle Cove thrived on.

A tiny octogenarian with an outsize presence, Gabby was dressed for the day in an exuberant green-and-white flowered print dress, her ever-present cane at her side and ready for battle. Though her manner could be off-putting (and yes, I mean rude), beneath her crusty exterior beat a heart of gold.

She held up a clipboard and shook it fiercely. "Have you double-checked with the event company when the folding chairs arrive?"

I restrained a sigh. Letting Gabby get hold of the to-do list for the upcoming Eagle Cove Flower Show had been a mistake. I wasn't the lead organizer — my mom was — but I'd agreed to help Mom out.

And Gabby had decided her job was to help me.

By hectoring me ceaselessly.

"The folding chairs arrive tomorrow morning," I said patiently.

"What about the tents?"

"Going up this afternoon on the Eagle Cove Common. The delivery trucks are on the way now. I'll be heading over after lunch. You should come with me."

She shook her head, not satisfied. "Cutting it pretty close to the bone."

"Everything's lining up nicely."

"What if a truck goes kaput on the drive over? One flat tire and you're toast."

"Nothing will happen to the trucks. Everything will be fine."

"Hope is not a plan. Emily wouldn't have left it to chance. She'd have a Plan B, Plan C — all the way to Plan Z."

I didn't disagree. For more than two decades, my Aunt Emily had headed up the flower show's organizing committee. Under her firm and expert guidance, the event had thrived.

But Emily was no longer available to run the show. Her funeral had put a stop to that.

I use that phrasing for a reason. Funerals are generally reserved for people who have died — but Emily was very much alive. After secretly surviving a terrifying car crash, she'd been declared legally dead and pulled back into service by H.U.S.H., the covert government agency she'd quit decades earlier.

Yes, improbable though it was, my eighty-four-year-old Aunt Emily was once again a spy.

One of the many consequences of her secret — and there were many, believe you me — was that the flower show had to move forward with someone else leading the charge.

"The tents are from the same company Emily used," I told Gabby. "We're following the same schedule she laid out."

Gabby scowled. "I still don't like it."

"Mom has a good handle on everything," I said loyally.

"Nancy's great, but Emily's the one who knew the score," Gabby shot back.

Again, I didn't disagree. Mom worked for the mayor and was perfectly capable of getting things done, and I was pretty good in that regard as well, but neither of us held a candle to Emily. "I'm sure everything will turn out fine."

Gabby gave the clipboard another shake. "Well, it better. The girls and I have a lot riding on this year's show."

"Tell me again what you're entering into competition."

From the booth, Mrs. Chan spoke up. "My

Lady Hillingdons — tea roses, Sarah — are doing wonderfully this year."

I appreciated Mrs. Chan's quick explanation of the flower she was talking about. Though I love all things floral, I'm no expert.

"My mopheads are looking great," said Mrs. Bunch.

"Mopheads?" I repeated.

"Hydrangeas, dear."

"This could be my year," Ms. Hollingsworth added. "My Golden Echoes — daffodils, dear — are coming along wonderfully."

Gabby's gang were a study in contrasts. Mrs. Chan, petite and composed, was dressed in a blue silk dress and pearls. Mrs. Bunch, short and solid, was sporting tan trousers and a white polo shirt and looked like she was heading to the golf course later, which she probably was. Ms. Hollingsworth, willowy and thin, was draped in a fluttery, watery blue-green dress that matched her breathy voice.

"We're locks for a win, all of us," Gabby said. "My Orange Pixie lilies are bursting with life force."

A lot like you, I almost said. "It sounds like you're all entering different categories?"

"Maximizing our chances."

"How many categories are there?"

Gabby batted the question away. "Who cares? What matters is we're gonna crush it."

"Thirty-two," Mr. Benson said from his spot at

the counter. "As has been the case for the past decade, the competition covers specialty classes in two main categories: arrangements and horticulture."

I glanced over. "Horticulture means ... potted flowers and plants?"

"Correct."

"I heard you're entering the orchid category?"

"*Trichocentrum cebolleta*. A truly breathtaking specimen. The finest I've ever cultivated."

"Snob," Gabby said from her booth.

Mr. Benson's back stiffened. Though he and Gabby were next-door neighbors and close friends, they enjoyed a vigorous tussle. "Snob?"

"All you orchid people," Gabby said breezily. "Snobs, snobs, snobs."

"That's not a fair —"

"Snooty patooties, every last one of you."

Mr. Benson adopted a patient air. "My dear, that's hardly —"

"Acting like you're the cream of the crop, tip of the top, king of the world, and for what? A repulsive, deformed flower."

A flush rose in his cheeks. "That's simply not —"

"Ugly and gross," she continued, aware she'd drawn blood. "Misshapen. Warped. *Weird*."

Finally roused to battle, Mr. Benson raised his voice. "Now listen here, woman —"

"Why should I? There's nothing to say. Everyone knows orchids are overrated."

"Clearly you're unfamiliar with the fascinating history of the orchid and its long, rich relationship with mankind —"

"You're saying you're in a *relationship* with that mutant flower of yours?"

"That's not what I —"

"Hate to break it to ya, old crank, but that weed doesn't know your name."

"That's not what —"

"The only thing it's thinking is, 'Gimme water. Turn me toward the sun. Stop snipping my leaves.'"

"Woman, if you're unable to appreciate the finer aspects of —"

"Can't face the truth, that it? How sad."

I was about to intervene when I was startled by a loud harrumph.

A man was standing at the cafe door, glaring at us.

"For land's sakes," the man thundered. "Will you ninnies ever cease your pointless caterwauling?"

CHAPTER 3

I stared at the interloper, unsure how to respond. He appeared to be in his seventies, with a plump build, a full head of white hair, and pale skin flushed with emotion. In his white suit, white shirt, white shoes, and blue bow tie, he looked like a courtly Southern gentleman, or perhaps a dandified chicken salesman.

A frown creased his pink forehead. "I expected better than this," he announced.

I still wasn't sure I'd heard correctly. "I'm sorry, what did you say?"

He turned his angry eyes toward me. "The back-country rusticity of this establishment may suit the preferences of the local denizens" — the way he said *denizens*, it was like he was referring to a rat infestation — "but you cannot expect me to wait for this rabble's mindless drivel to dribble to a merciful close. The manner in which I choose to live my life is more elevated and refined."

The entire cafe gaped at him, stupefied into silence — even Gabby, who generally refused to take guff of any sort.

Clearly aware of his audience, the man stepped to the display counter for a closer look at Janie's delicious pies, muffins, and scones. "How sadly typical."

"I'm sorry?" I said.

"These baked goods. The lack of imagination. Generic, commodified, plebeian." He sniffed the air, as if hoping to locate an unplebeian aroma. "I suppose I shouldn't be surprised."

There was something almost comical about this unpleasant man. Did he really think it was okay to be so insulting? To be so unnecessarily rude to complete strangers?

"If you don't like what you see, you don't have to stay," I said, trying to keep my tone level.

"Ah, but I do. Sadly."

"I'm not sure what you mean."

"That much is obvious." He plucked a piece of paper from his coat pocket. "Summon your manager."

"My manager?" I repeated, trying to decide how offended I should be.

"Her name is Sarah Boone. She has prepared an apartment for me."

I restrained a groan as the puzzle piece snapped into place. "You're a judge for the flower show. Professor Beauregard Greeley."

He puffed out his chest. "Head judge, yes."

"I'm Sarah Boone, manager of Emily's Eats and owner of the studio apartment you'll be staying in during your time here in Eagle Cove."

He seemed unimpressed. "Well?"

My eyebrows rose. "Well, what?"

"When you've finished your long-winded introduction, show me to my room."

Swallowing my anger, I pointed to the door leading from the cafe to the building's hallway. "Through there."

Before following him into the hallway, I popped my head into the kitchen to confer with Janie. "Can you watch the register for a few minutes?"

"Of course," she said, her gaze sympathetic.

"I take it you saw?"

"And heard."

I grabbed the studio apartment keys from a drawer below the cash register, then met the professor in the hallway and gestured to the stairs. "One flight up."

"No elevator?"

"Stairs only."

With an annoyed huff, he headed up, moving easily despite his roly-poly build.

"The studio apartment is at the end of the hall. The door's unlocked."

After surveying the door with distaste, he gripped the handle, pushed the door open, and let out a disappointed sigh. Though the studio is small, I keep it well-maintained, much like an upscale hotel room.

"Cramped and dismal," he pronounced.

That's when my first ~~murderous~~ musing manifested. I imagined him flying off a steep cliff — maybe pushed, maybe not, I admit nothing! — before plummeting to a well-deserved demise.

The delightfulness of this deathly vision fortified me enough to hold back from responding to his critique — barely. "I hope after settling in you find it comfortable."

"I will require room service immediately."

"There is no room service." Willing myself to remain calm, I handed him the keys and a business card. "Feel free to call or come down to the cafe if you any have questions."

He stared at the card. "This is unacceptable."

"The cafe opens at seven-thirty and closes at five. On Main Street, there are several nice restaurants within walking distance, including Mario's across the street."

"Does this establishment at least provide extra towels?"

"I can get you some."

"Ms. Boone, this will not do."

I nearly said *too bad* but managed to hold my tongue. "I should get going. If there's anything I can help with, please feel free to come down to the cafe or call."

"Is that the sum of your response? To look at me and say, 'I should get going?'"

I took a deep breath. The last thing I wanted was for my big mouth to cause trouble. Mom and Mayor Johnson had been super-excited about Professor Greeley agreeing to be a judge. He was a highly regarded horticulture expert, they'd said. He was a big "get" for our little show, they'd said.

"Professor," I said, struggling to maintain an even tone. "I'm happy to help you in any way I can. I'll bring you the extra towels and I'm a quick call away if you have any questions."

"Meaningless twaddle."

"Then what do you want?"

"Action." He gestured around. "This room is an abomination."

"It's the only room available."

He harrumphed. "I suppose, as far as you're concerned, that settles it?"

I could only stare at him. "I don't know what to say. If you don't want to stay here, you don't have to."

"Young lady, the last place I want is to be is *here*,

attempting to explain the basics of customer service to the likes of you."

"Then why are you here?" I finally snapped. "Why did you agree to come to Eagle Cove and judge our flower show?"

"That is none of your concern."

I should have let it go — really, I should have — but found myself adding, "I mean, since you're so refined and all."

His eyes widened in shock. "I expect to be treated with *respect*."

"You get what you give," I shot back.

"What is worthy of respect here?" he said incredulously, waving his arms around. "Surely you cannot expect me to lower my standards and pretend to be impressed with the so-called charms of this dreary backwater?"

It took every effort to hold back my anger. "Professor Greeley, I have a suggestion. Let's agree that you and I don't have to pretend to like each other. But I hope you'll be nicer to the other folks here in Eagle Cove, many of whom are quite excited to welcome you."

"Folks like you, I suppose?" he sneered. "Rude, unrefined, tiresome *folks* like you?"

I swallowed, stunned. "I don't know what I've done or said to offend you."

"You are northern trash," he declared. "Through and through. It gives me no pleasure saying this." Then he puffed out his chest, clearly bursting with pleasure. "The art of hospitality is a tradition of which you are sadly ignorant."

"Enjoy your stay, Professor."

I was almost out the door when he said, "Ms. Boone."

I almost didn't stop. "Yes, Professor?"

"Have the bellman bring up my trunk."

I froze. "Trunk?"

"On the curb."

"We don't have a bellman."

He looked me up and down. "Then any common laborer will do."

CHAPTER 4

There's probably a special place reserved in you-know-where for you-know-whats like Professor Greeley. At least I hope there is.

Well, maybe I don't actually hope that. Condemning a human being to eternal torment for the crime of being gratuitously mean doesn't seem quite right. The proportionality is perhaps, maybe, just ever-so-slightly, out of whack.

But a nice long stay? A week or two of unrelenting discomfort? Enough pain and suffering for Professor Sourpuss to realize how badly he was behaving and come begging for forgiveness?

Yes, a week of brimstone and fire sounded perfect.

Those thoughts and many others raced through my head as I shut the studio door and headed downstairs. After going outside to confirm the professor's trunk was indeed on the sidewalk, I grabbed the dolly from the cafe's storage room and rolled it outside. With the entire gang in the cafe watching through the front window, mouths agape, I maneuvered the professor's ornate steamer trunk onto the dolly, then lugged it up the stairs and into the studio apartment.

"I will charge the flower show if I find any damage," the professor sniffed as I headed out.

"You do that," I said, seething.

"You are a disgrace."

Then he slammed the door — angrily, loudly, ostentatiously — in my face.

I stared at the door, practically breathing fire, taking deep breaths in an unsuccessful attempt to calm myself down.

Through my red mist of rage, I retained enough sense to realize that my professor-related trials had only begun. The instant I returned to the cafe, an army of small-town interrogators would swarm over me and, with precision and skill, ruthlessly extract every morsel of information about our encounter. I'd be poked and prodded until they bled me dry.

Before I subjected myself to that inevitable barrage, it behooved me to get my head on straight. My concern wasn't the professor — *him* I'd throw to the wolves without blinking. No, my concern was Mom. As lead organizer for the flower show, she had a lot on her plate. The last thing she needed was her daughter fanning the flames of righteous rage against her head judge.

Which meant just one thing: A detour was required. A chance to decompress and let off steam. I knew exactly what I needed. With eagerness in my steps, I dashed up the stairs to my apartment on the third floor. Once inside, I whipped out my phone and dialed a very familiar number.

"Hey, Sarah," a deep voice rumbled in my ear. "What's up?"

I sighed with pleasure and relief. The voice belonged to Matt Forsyth, Eagle Cove's sheriff and the handsome fellow I happened to be dating.

I gave him a quick rundown of everything the bad professor had put me through.

"Can I evict him?" I pleaded. "Haul him downstairs, kick him to the curb, and banish him forever?"

He chuckled. "Sorry you have to deal with him, Sarah. He's definitely a handful."

Already I felt myself calming down. Matt's voice was so comforting. I'd always loved the way he said my name.

"Why is he being so completely insufferable?" I continued, still in vent mode. "Everything he said was so over-the-top."

"Totally agree."

That's when I realized he'd implied something.

"Wait, it sounds like you already know what he's like."

Now it was Matt's turn to sigh. "The mayor asked if a deputy could drive the professor from the train station in Middlemore, so I sent Deputy Wilkerson."

"That was very accommodating of you."

"When Wilkerson arrived, the professor said he expected to be greeted by a limousine, not a 'beaten-down dirty truck.'"

"Oh, geez."

"Then he demanded proof that Wilkerson was old enough to drive."

I laughed incredulously. Deputy Paul was in his early twenties and looked younger than his age, but *come on*.

"The good professor complained nonstop the entire drive. The road had too many curves. His seat belt didn't fit. The flower show was too small and unimportant for the likes of him."

At that point, I uttered what some might consider an inappropriate word.

Matt laughed. "Exactly."

"Well, the weekend won't last forever," I said, trying to console myself. "Soon enough we'll be rid of him forever."

"That's the spirit." He cleared his throat. "Listen, while I have you, can I ask about the opening reception?"

"Sure," I said, mentally shifting gears. "What do you need to know?"

"I know you and Janie are catering. But give me the high-level overview again."

"It's two days from now — Thursday afternoon — from one to three in a tent on the Common. A hundred guests are expected. Dress is spring attire. In addition to wine, champagne, and tea, we're serving appetizers inspired by English afternoon teas."

"The event's ticketed, right?"

"Invitation-only for the organizers, judges, media, and selected guests. Why do you ask?"

"The mayor asked for my input on how to keep out gatecrashers."

"Ah," I said, beginning to follow. "Mom mentioned something about that. Apparently, several competitors snuck into last year's reception. They thought face time with the judges would increase their chances of winning 'best-of-show' ribbons for their flower entries."

"How's your mom planning to handle that this year?"

"I believe the tents this year have canvas side flaps that extend all the way to the ground, which means it may be possible to keep folks from slipping in from the sides."

"Got it. Speaking of, your mom called. I should get back to her."

"The tents are going up this afternoon. I'll be heading over later to check them out, and Janie and I will be there tonight to get started on the setup. Will I see you there?"

"Definitely. After I get back from Middlemore."

"Ah, that's right." Matt's two teenaged sons were heading to Boston to visit their mom and Matt was driving them to the train station in Middlemore. "Give the boys my best."

"Will do. Talk with you later?"

"Later!"

CHAPTER 5

I set the phone down, reassured and restored. Nearly a quarter century after I fell in love with Matt in high school and broke up with him in college, the two of us were dating again. And I had to admit — things were going well. We were like excited kids again, eager for each and every moment we managed to steal for ourselves amidst the many responsibilities of our busy lives.

I took a deep breath. Just hearing his voice had soothed me. My urge to throttle a certain bad professor had almost entirely subsided.

I was about to return to the cafe for my inevitable interrogation when I heard a familiar scratching from the kitchen. With a smile, I watched Mr. Snuggles, my curious and confident tabby pal, emerge from the old dumbwaiter shaft in the kitchen wall. The shaft, an original feature of the building, ran from the basement to the top floor and served as Mr. Snuggles's primary means of moving from apartment to apartment. How he managed to travel up and down in the shaft was beyond me, but my feline friend made it look easy.

With athletic ease, he hopped from the kitchen counter and sauntered toward me.

"Well, hello there," I said, bending down to scratch his ears. "How are you doing today?"

He looked up at me inquisitively, then rubbed himself against my legs and purred loudly. I knew exactly what he wanted — he'd trained me well — so I made a beeline for the rocking chair next to the front window and sat down.

The instant my rear hit the rocker, Mr. Snuggles jumped onto my legs.

"You are such a dear," I murmured as he stepped closer and pressed his nose into my chin. "So friendly."

He purred again, holding my gaze for a long moment, then settled into my lap.

And just like that, I was trapped. Happily so. The chair, a classic Boston rocker with a spindled back, felt wonderful against my sore shoulders. The front window offered a view of Main Street below and, in the distance, the forested ridge rising above Eagle Cove.

The view was one of the many things I loved about this apartment. I'd moved in soon after Aunt

Emily "died" and willed the place to me. I now considered myself its caretaker, thankful and appreciative for the chance to live here until Emily returned. There was a graciousness to these well-proportioned, beautifully furnished rooms that spoke to me. Aside from adding a few family photos, I hadn't changed a thing.

In my lap, Mr. Snuggles was looking up at me like he knew what I was thinking. *Don't go downstairs yet*, he seemed to be saying. *You've been running nonstop. You deserve a break. Rub my belly.*

"You are such a sweetheart," I murmured, rubbing his belly as ordered. "What would I do without you?"

I thought about the word I'd uttered: *sweetheart*. An innocent-enough word when describing a cat, but a bit more loaded when referring to the certain someone I happened to be dating.

With a sigh, I looked through the window toward the forested ridge and allowed my mind to go where it clearly wanted to go.

I've had two sweethearts — two loves — in my life. The first was Matt. We met in my junior year of high school and were together until my sophomore year of college — until the moment when, in the mistaken belief that I was being realistic and practical, I foolishly ended our long-distance relationship.

The second love of my life was the man I met in college and divorced last year.

I haven't discussed Ethan much yet. I haven't wanted to. The pain he caused in the final years of our marriage was still too close — too fresh, too raw, too difficult. My move to Eagle Cove had been driven in part by my need for a clean break from the turmoil that ended our union. Staying busy — working nonstop, pushing myself past my limits — had helped keep the past at bay.

But as I was reluctantly beginning to acknowledge, avoidance only gets one so far.

Little by little, piece by piece, my past was coming back to confront me.

If I wanted to start anew, I would have to examine my pain.

The reason for that reckoning was tall, dark, and ruggedly handsome. The reason set my heart racing every time he stepped into the cafe.

So let me start with the obvious: I have a type. Both Matt and Ethan are that type — tall, attractive, athletic guys. They're also smart and confident — qualities I respond to (ahem) as well.

Ethan entered my life in the fall of my senior year of college. He saw me across a crowded room at a house party and waded through a packed dance floor to introduce himself. The chemistry between us was immediate and powerful. Not only was he my type — the aforementioned tall/handsome/smart/confident — he was ambitious, outgoing, and charming. He told me he wanted to go places, and I found myself wondering what it would be like to go with him. For the better part of the fall semester he pursued me; eventually I allowed myself to be caught. Our whirlwind romance was heady, exhilarating, and hopelessly rushed. A month before graduation, he proposed. We married that fall and moved to L.A., where he dove into real estate and eventually established his own successful brokerage. I worked at a small advertising agency until, two short years later, we were blessed with the arrival of our daughter, Anna. I stayed home (mostly happily) until Anna started first grade, then took a job in the fraud department at a bank.

The two of us had our share of disagreements — we're both strong-willed individuals who like to get our way— but for fifteen of our twenty years of marriage we were happy. Our daughter was thriving. We loved each other. I believed with all my heart that we were in it together for the long haul.

The unraveling began when he landed a listing for a beachfront property in Malibu. The owner was an executive at a movie studio. For the first time in his real-estate career, Ethan was dealing with entertainment types. He found he loved their brashness, savvy, and ambition. Their energy spoke to him, he told me.

I was considerably less keen. When he dragged me to "industry" parties, I met people who were smart and ambitious, yes, but also insecure and insincere. Gossip was their currency. Everything revolved around "deals." If you were able to help them, they adored you. If you couldn't, you barely existed. Try as I might, I couldn't fathom the appeal. What was so special about making a movie or TV show? Why did the process require so much unpleasantness? Why were so many in the industry willing to participate in — and perpetuate — a system so lacking in basic human decency?

But Ethan wouldn't be deterred. He wanted to get into "content," as he called it. Without telling me, he invested in a production company. When I found out and raised concerns, he became resentful. And I, in turn, grew worried.

For a while, he tried selling me on his vision. When he realized I wasn't going to ever see things his way, he began cutting me out of the loop. I responded by minimizing what was happening, trying to convince myself that the distance between us wasn't worrisome, even as more of his time and energy went toward his new passion.

As our lives grew increasingly separate, I blamed myself for the slow unraveling of our once-close bond. I was too risk-averse, I chastised myself. Why couldn't I be more optimistic, more imaginative, more open? Why couldn't I find faith that his drive and ambition — the same qualities he'd brought to his real-estate business — could lead to success in entertainment?

The end, when it came, was sudden and sharp. To my shock, I discovered he'd tapped into Anna's college fund to invest in a stupid reality TV show. Furious and hurt, I confronted him. Rather than apologize, he went on the offensive. I didn't get what he was trying to do, he told me, and he was afraid I never would.

Then he upped the ante — going where I'd feared to tread.

I need a wife who supports me, he said.

I need a husband who doesn't risk his daughter's future, I shot back.

I'm investing in her future.

The only person you're fooling is yourself.

From my years at the bank, I knew the smell of financial malfeasance. What Ethan was doing stank to high heaven.

So with Anna's future in mind, I opened new bank accounts in my name and moved most of our remaining savings out of the joint accounts. And then, after a long weekend of crying my eyes out, I hired the best lawyer I could and filed for separation.

Eighteen expensive months later, our marriage came to a painful end.

Ethan lives in Malibu now. I'm told he's dating

an actress. His production company is gaining a
foothold in the entertainment industry, according to
the "trades," with several TV "projects" completed
and others announced for production.

Financial matters aside, he's largely been a good
father to Anna. They remain close. During the
divorce, I tried my best to shield Anna from the
worst of it, and I'm relieved to report that I
managed to hold my tongue, at least for the most
part.

Over the past year, my life has changed in just
about every way imaginable. Anna left the nest for
college. I sold the house in L.A. and moved back to
Eagle Cove. I'm the co-owner of a cafe and
working harder than I ever have. Aside from
missing my daughter like crazy, I'm mostly very
happy about where I am and what I'm doing.

But I'm still carrying the burden and scars of
my failed marriage.

Which brings me to Matt.

I have baggage. Heavy, unwieldy baggage —
not the kind with wheels for easy movement. Mine
takes real elbow grease to move. Mine can't be
maneuvered onto a dolly and lugged up the stairs.

Matt's life is already overloaded. His sheriff's
job is demanding. He's raising two high-school-age
sons. The last thing he needs is me dumping my
pain on him. The last thing he wants is me exposing
him to my lingering anger and hurt.

He deserves better from me — much better.

So until my past is truly in my past, I'm taking things slowly.

And he's fine with that, mostly. He's been through a divorce as well — he knows the territory. Sometimes, when he looks at me with his deep brown eyes, I think he understands my fears better than I do.

Still, every now and then, I sense his impatience. He wants a future with me. I want the same with him.

Someday, when I'm ready, I might allow that future to happen.

CHAPTER 6

After indulging Mr. Snuggles a few minutes more, I eased him from my lap and returned to the cafe, where (as expected) the gang vigorously pumped me for dirt on Professor Sourface. Thankfully, I managed to avoid handing over any fresh ammo. I told them the professor continued to behave rudely — Gabby and her crew needed something to chew on, after all — but left out the bits where he called me "northern trash" and Eagle Cove a "dreary backwater."

That afternoon, after the cafe's daily rush had faded to a trickle and with Janie holding down the fort while awaiting delivery of a crucial ingredient, I set out for the quick walk to the Common. The air was fresh and mild, the sky clear and blue, the sun lovely on my cheeks as I strolled past the restaurants, shops, and local businesses that make up Eagle Cove's downtown. Most of the buildings date to the late 1800s and retain their Victorian-era appeal — a big draw for tourists who flock here throughout the year. I felt a rush of gratitude that once again I was able to call this place home.

The Common is a wide-open grassy expanse between downtown and Heartsprings Lake. After a frigid winter blanketed in snow, its lawn was now a rich, vibrant green. Three big tents for the flower show were already up, their white canvas crisp and cheerful in the afternoon sun.

The tents looked huge as I approached — so tall and spacious. Everywhere I looked, volunteers were dashing to and fro — installing lights, hanging up signs, testing the sound system. I couldn't help but admire their energy as they set about their tasks.

Inside one of the tents, the show's lead organizer was directing the action, clipboard in hand. Most folks know the organizer as Nancy Boone, the social dynamo with the sparkling green eyes and stylish auburn bob who lights up any room she's in. But to me she's simply Mom.

As office manager for the mayor, Mom's great at getting things done and getting people involved. And now, as the head of the flower show's organizing committee, those skills were being put to the test.

In two short days, thousands of horticulture enthusiasts would descend on Eagle Cove to enjoy the beauty of some of nature's most delightful offerings. The competition would feature flower arrangements and individual plants from hundreds of contestants, all of them hoping to win Best of Show ribbons and the show's grand prize, the Golden Pot.

"Good, you're here," Mom said as I neared. "The reception tent went up a little while ago. Let's do a walk-through."

She set off at a rapid pace, with me hustling to keep up.

"The tables arrive at three," she said as we walked. "The folding chairs will be here tomorrow morning." She glanced at her clipboard with an anxious frown. "Or is that the other way around?"

"It's okay, Mom. You've got this."

"I hope so," she said with a sigh. "If only Emily…."

"I know."

"Well, there's nothing to do about that. The show must go on."

When we reached the tent, I found myself smiling. The space felt light and welcoming, the white canvas soaring above us and glowing under the sun. Canvas side flaps extended all the way to the ground and seemed to envelope the space in a gentle hug.

"This tent should do quite nicely for the reception, right?" Mom asked.

"It looks perfect." I pulled out my phone and started snapping photos to share with Janie. "The entrance where you check the tickets will be…?"

"There," she said, pointing to a spot on one side of the tent.

"And the stage will be…?"

"At the far end. It's a raised platform with a lectern and a table for panelists."

She took me through the proposed layout for the opening reception, pointing out the spots for the serving stations and flower display pedestals. "We'll also have tables and chairs sprinkled about for guests who want to sit, though we expect most folks will move around and circulate."

"This looks terrific. A lovely spot for an afternoon party."

"I hope so. Any menu issues?"

"Nothing to worry about. Janie had a close call with one of the ingredients — a certain type of flour — but she found a place that has what she needs and they're delivering to the cafe in a bit."

"And the serving staff?"

"All lined up and ready to go."

She was about to ask another question when something caught her eye. "Ah, good. I can introduce you."

I pivoted and saw two women approaching, white and probably in their sixties. The taller of the two, dressed in dark slacks and a light blue blouse under a long black coat, wore her gray hair short and seemed like the type who enjoyed being in charge of something. Her companion, tiny and bird-like with flowing, vaguely hippie-ish white hair, was dressed in blue jeans and a cream linen blouse with a chunky turquoise necklace.

"Harriet and Polly," Mom said brightly. "I'd like to introduce you to my daughter Sarah."

I realized the two women were Harriet Vale and Polly Pence, two of the judges for the flower show. "Welcome to Eagle Cove," I said as we shook hands. "Pleased to meet you both."

Mom jumped in. "Sarah's cafe — Emily's Eats on Main Street, you may have seen it — is catering the opening reception."

Harriet, the taller of the two, nodded. "We noticed the cafe this morning. Polly and I went for a walk through your downtown to acquaint ourselves with Eagle Cove. We almost went in, but you seemed quite busy."

"It gets a little crazy during the morning rush, but it quiets down in the afternoon."

"Sarah, did you say?" Polly said with a smile. "Someone mentioned your cafe. They told us your muffins are delicious."

"I'm so glad to hear that. My co-owner Janie is an amazing baker. Please swing by anytime."

"We'll do that."

Polly was about to say more when she spotted

something over my shoulder and inhaled sharply. I turned and saw Mayor Johnson and my new favorite person, Professor Greeley, walking across the Common toward the tent furthest from us, the mayor talking and the professor looking displeased.

"Excuse us," Harriet said abruptly. "We have an appointment. Nice to meet you, Sarah."

And with that, the two women hurried off.

Oh, dear, I thought as they dashed away. They'd been about as subtle as a tank. "Mom, what's the deal?"

She sighed. "Professor Greeley is a last-minute replacement for a judge who got sick. When Polly and Harriet found out he was coming, they nearly canceled."

"Whoa."

"Doris had to talk them into staying. We had to promise to keep him separated from them as much as possible."

Which explained the mayor steering the professor away from us and toward another tent. "Any idea why?"

Mom shrugged. "I assume it's something from the flower show circuit. It's a small world. All of them are highly regarded judges. Though I suspect there's more."

I was about to ask her to elaborate when it became my turn to have my attention diverted. In the tent next to ours, I spied a man I recognized.

Tall, fit, Black, and in his thirties, he had a video camera on his shoulder and was interviewing one of the volunteers.

Two thoughts came: What was Edgar doing here? And what did Mom know?

I gestured toward him. "Who's that with the video camera?"

She swung around. "Oh, that's Edgar, our event videographer."

"Videographer?"

"You know, documenting the show for the website and social media."

"I thought you hired Gerry for that."

"We did, but at the last minute he got an extremely lucrative contract gig in Boston that he couldn't pass up. He recommended Edgar."

I kept my expression neutral. *Of course Gerry got a huge gig out of nowhere that allowed Edgar to quickly take his place.* "Glad you were able to find a replacement so quickly."

"Oh, Edgar's been so helpful — a godsend, really. We had an issue with the sound system earlier and he jumped right in and fixed it."

She doesn't know, I realized. "Glad to hear. Sounds like a great hire."

At that moment, a volunteer called Mom's name and waved her over. Mom frowned. "Sarah, I have to deal with the backup generator. Is it okay if I…?"

"Of course. I'm going to take a few more pics here and get back to the cafe. Janie will be swinging by later to check out the space."

"The two of you will be here tomorrow evening to start setup?"

"Yep. With final setup first thing Thursday morning."

"Call me if anything comes up?"

"Right away. Promise."

"Thank you, dear." As I watched her hurry away with the volunteer, I felt a sense of relief. Despite the stress, she seemed to have things under control.

I snapped a few more photos in the tent while deciding on my next move. Then, after taking a deep breath, I made my way to Edgar, reaching him just as he wrapped up his video interview with the volunteer.

He'd already seen me, of course. "Good afternoon, Sarah," he said with a friendly smile.

A few months back, he'd been working as a security guard. Or pretending to be. .

"Videographer?" I said. "A man of many talents."

He shrugged. "I like to keep busy."

"Fixing the sound system?"

Another shrug. "Happy to help."

"You aren't here to help."

"I'm not?"

I lowered my voice. "What's going on, Edgar? What possible interest could H.U.S.H. have in a flower show?"

He gave me a look of mild reproof. "You said you were going to forget that name."

"Oops, my bad. Come on, what gives?"

"Maybe I really like roses."

"Don't take this the wrong way, but seeing you worries me. Every time your super-secret spy agency starts sniffing around Eagle Cove, people wind up dead."

A teasing smile came to his lips. "Sarah, I'm just here for the flowers."

His answer told me three things: He knew I knew he was lying, he didn't care that I knew he knew I knew he was lying, and he wasn't going to tell me anything.

Spies and their secrets. *Grrrr*. I tried a different tactic. "I hope you know you can trust me."

"Of course."

"What's with the Mona Lisa smile?"

The smile turned into a big grin, lighting up his handsome face. "Sorry."

I sighed. The thing was, I liked Edgar. My gut told me he was a good sort and just doing his job — a job that had zero to do with me.

Be grateful you're out of the loop, I told myself. *Ignorance is bliss.*

"Can you promise me that everything's okay?"

He shrugged. "That's really not how things work."

I looked around. "Any of your pals here?"

The Mona Lisa smile returned. "Sometimes I prefer to go solo."

Grrrr. But I got the message. "Okay, fine, I get it. Secret spy business blah blah blah. But if anything comes up I should know about...."

He nodded, his expression becoming serious. "You'll be the first to hear."

CHAPTER 7

I left the Common and headed back to the cafe, mulling what I'd learned.

Edgar's presence made clear that someone or something at the flower show was of interest to H.U.S.H.

But who or what? And why?

Needless to say, I had concerns. Twice in the past seven months, spies had infiltrated Eagle Cove in search of secrets. People had died. Others I cared about — me included — had been put in harm's way.

Was danger close at hand again?

By the time I reached the cafe, I was on the verge of becoming rather cross with H.U.S.H. for deliberately choosing to keep me out of the loop, and I was contemplating possible ways to squeeze the info out of them when I was stopped in my tracks by what I saw through the cafe window.

Professor Greeley had returned from the Common and was holding court inside.

As soon as I opened the door, I realized "holding court" was hardly the right description for the verbal assault under way.

"No," the professor was saying, his puffed-out chest bursting with pride, "the concerns I have with miserable third-tier flower shows like yours go far beyond the deplorable quality of the competition entries."

Oh, dear.

For the second time that day, the entire cafe was gaping at him in silence, mesmerized again by his gratuitous and over-the-top insults. From the register, Janie shot me a distressed look. On his stool at the counter, Mr. Benson's mouth hung open. Gabby and her gang were staring from their booth, faces flushed with shock.

The professor, meanwhile, was thoroughly enjoying himself.

"Nor," he continued, "do I waste time on the deluded fools who believe their inferior floral specimens are worthy of honor and glory. Those pathetic souls are merely a reflection of the undemanding era in which we live, in which standards have vanished, ignorance is endemic, and rubbish is the new norm."

He let out a loud sigh. "Lamentably, it has become apparent that my lot in life, my tragic burden, if you will, is to bear proud witness to the demise of a once-great horticultural tradition, a tradition shaped by guardians like myself who kept the unfiltered hordes at bay in favor of those few who possessed the proper knowledge, discernment, and pedigree."

"Hordes?" I said, unable to stop myself.

All eyes swung to me, including the professor's.

"Ms. Boone," he said, practically licking his lips with anticipation. "I see you've returned from your dilatory jaunt."

"My what?" I said, taken aback.

"Dereliction of duty is the term I would use if I believed you capable of comprehending even basic notions of service. But alas."

I stared at him, truly baffled. What was he talking about?

"I refer, Ms. Boone, to your aimless strolling, to your indulging in vapid chatter while your so-called business" — he looked around the cafe and sniffed with disdain — "flounders."

Ah. So much to unpack there. Starting with: He'd seen me at the Common talking with Polly and Harriet and didn't like it.

"Well, Professor," I said, relieved to hear my voice sounding calm, even though I wanted to throw my shoe at him. "I'll admit I'm surprised. I mean, given your refined tastes and all, I would have thought the 'unfiltered hordes' — charter member here, by the way — would be unworthy of your attention."

He sighed again. "Such misplaced pride. Reveling in your ignorance. How I pity you."

"How can this horde member help you, Professor?"

He frowned. "There was a time when impertinence such as yours would have been dealt with."

"Can I get you a muffin or a latte? Do you need directions somewhere? Maybe more towels? Or are you just here to pontificate to a captive audience?"

I heard a gasp from the booth — Mrs. Chan, I think, though I wasn't looking her way and couldn't be sure.

The professor's cheeks flushed. I'd gotten to him. "Ms. Boone, your behavior is appalling. In all my years, I have never encountered such rudeness."

Bunk, I almost said. *In all your years, I bet tons of folks have gotten a whiff of your spew and told you to zip it.*

But instead — and to this day, I don't know how — I held my tongue. Or rather, I prevented my tongue from saying more. I'd like to say I accomplished that herculean feat because, as a responsible cafe owner, I understood the importance of maintaining one's poise when dealing with difficult customers. More likely, I did it only because of Mom — not wanting to cause more trouble for her and the flower show.

"You know what," I said, the words feeling gritty in my mouth. "That last sentence of mine was neither appropriate nor helpful. The bit about you pontificating, I mean. I apologize for that."

The professor kept his glare going, clearly wanting more, clearly hoping I'd fall to my knees and beg for forgiveness, wailing and crying and gnashing my teeth.

Instead I held his stare and waited for him to blink.

Which he finally did. "Unbelievable," he said, shaking his head. "I chose to enter this" — he seemed to be searching for a neutral word — "*establishment* in the spirit of generosity and beneficence bestowed upon me by my forebears, guided by the hope, slim and tenuous I grant, that I might discover something edible amongst these commonplace offerings."

Beneficence? I willed myself not to laugh.

He sniffed the air, then turned his glare back on. "Now I've lost my appetite."

And with that he stormed out of the cafe.

The second the door shut behind him, the place erupted into a cacophony of outrage.

"That man," Mr. Benson said, struggling for the right words, "is deeply disturbed."

"What a tool!" Gabby thundered.

As I watched him march down Main Street, full of vigor and spite, I noticed Hialeah across the street, hurrying away in the opposite direction.

And I remembered something. That morning, while I was maneuvering the professor's steamer trunk onto the dolly, Hialeah hadn't been among those watching through the cafe window. She'd been in her favorite seat by the window a few minutes earlier, when the professor first appeared. But by the time I'd come back downstairs, she'd vanished.

CHAPTER 8

Looking back, it's fair to describe the Wednesday before the opening reception as the calm before the storm — if one can define "calm" as a frenetic, nonstop whirl of event preparation. Janie and I shut the cafe at noon to devote our afternoon to getting everything ready. Not only was the reception our first big catering gig, it was also super-high-profile. The pressure was on to deliver a flawless event.

Despite weeks of careful planning, we still had a million things to check off our task list. I was on my hands and knees in front of the display counter, trying to figure out the right way to set champagne flutes in their container to ensure they didn't break during the drive to the reception tent, when Gabby and Mr. Benson popped in to show off the flowers they were entering into the competition.

I glanced up briefly. Each held a potted plant and seemed proud and excited. I'll confess I barely took in their floral treasures before saying, "Oh, my, yes, so lovely."

"We're walking them over to the Common," Mr. Benson said. "Taking advantage of the beautiful weather."

"I hope you both win," I said as I tried positioning the flutes in the box a different way.

"You know, Gabby," Mr. Benson said as they turned to leave, "I should have mentioned this sooner. Your lily might benefit from a different pot for the competition. I have a pot that would work quite well."

"What do you mean?" Gabby said, immediately on the defensive.

Interest piqued, I looked up and saw that Mr. Benson was right. Gabby's clay pot was large and bulky — way too chunky for the tiny plant it held. Also, she'd hand-painted it a garish kaleidoscope of red, yellow, green, purple, and white.

"Well," Mr. Benson said, attempting to be diplomatic. "Your lily might stand out more in a pot that's smaller and less … colorful."

Gabby waved off the suggestion. "Nah."

"I'm only trying to help."

"What do you know about color, old man? The only colors you like are gray and taupe."

"Now listen here, woman —"

"Guys," I said, hoping to head off their imminent squabble. "I'm sorry, but Janie and I need to focus. Would you mind if…?"

"Of course, Sarah." Mr. Benson stepped to the hallway door and held it open for Gabby. "If Gabby wants to distract the judges from the beauty of her flower with that eyesore of a pot, that is her prerogative."

"Can the commentary, you old crank," Gabby said as she swept past him. "Just you wait. This little cutie's gonna crush it."

"Thanks for coming by," I said quickly. "And good luck!"

And then it was back to the whirl of preparation. For the next two hours, Janie and I worked steadily and made a nice-size dent in our task list. Sometime around four, we gave ourselves a short break to deal with personal errands before beginning the next round of prep. "Back in thirty," Janie said as she hurried out the door. "Sounds good," I replied, grateful for the chance to take a breath and regroup.

Grabbing the clipboard, I reviewed our to-do list. We'd made progress, yes, but what had we missed? Almost immediately, I zoomed in on one of my many uncompleted tasks: calling each of the folks we'd hired as servers to make sure they knew what to wear and where and when to arrive tomorrow. I flipped the page, expecting to find the contact list, then frowned when I realized I'd left it in the apartment.

With a sigh, I dashed upstairs and was hurrying past the studio apartment on the second floor when I heard the murmur of voices inside — the professor's querulous tones and, more faintly, those of a woman.

I froze in my tracks, my curiosity immediately revving into high gear. Who could that be? Who would willingly spend time with that awful man?

Fully aware that my nosiness was indefensible for all kinds of reasons, not least of which was my utter lack of time to indulge in anything other than the mountain of work awaiting me downstairs, I stepped closer and placed my ear against the door. Though I could distinguish between the professor and the woman, I still couldn't make out what they were saying.

Time for Plan B. As quietly as possible, I crept up the stairs to the third floor and dropped to my hands and knees next to the railing. From here I could peer through the slats in the railing and avoid being seen by those below.

Inside the studio apartment, the muffled conversation continued. A minute passed, then two. I began feeling a tad foolish. Why was I doing this? Nosiness wasn't exactly a virtue. It was none of my business who Professor Snobface was talking to. Plus, I had gobs of work to do.

Still I waited, feeling sillier by the second.

I was about to give up when the door clicked open and the visitor stepped out. To my shock, I saw it was Claire Emerson, my childhood best friend. Dressed in black slacks and a light cream sweater, her blond hair in a stylish bob, she looked as sleek and gorgeous as usual.

Ever-so-carefully, my mind awhirl, I inched away from the railing to avoid being seen.

A bit of background before going further. Claire and I grew up in Eagle Cove and as kids were inseparable best friends. But after college we grew apart. For nearly twenty years, I didn't understand why — until I learned that Claire had followed Aunt Emily into the world of espionage and now worked with Emily (and Edgar) as a spy. I'd found this out the previous fall, shortly before Claire and I were almost murdered by a ruthless assassin. Since then, the two of us had been working to mend our long-frayed friendship.

I heard the professor's voice. "You better —"

"Just do your part," Claire said.

"Your lack of respect —"

"Is the least of your concerns." Her voice had an edge. "You were reactivated for one reason. Stay focused on that."

I nearly gasped out loud. *Reactivated?* Professor Sourface was a *former spy*? Not only was this mind-boggling, it was also completely delicious. I found myself wishing I could see his face.

"Young lady," the professor spluttered. "It is not your place to —"

"No," Claire said, her tone icy. "Stop right there. It is my place. It is, in fact, my responsibility."

"You have no right —"

"I have every right. I'm hearing things about your behavior, Professor. Bad things. Reports of you insulting people, offending people, alienating people."

"Stirring the pot is a well-understood technique, young lady."

"Only when the pot is the target. Only when you know who added the ingredients. Only when you know who's hungry. None of that applies in this case."

He snorted. "Since when do we care about offending the local yokels?"

"Reason One: I grew up here. These yokels, as you call them, are my friends."

"I see. There are correctives for that."

Claire's tone sharpened. "Meaning?"

"You've allowed yourself to be taken in. Your sentimental loyalties are blinding you to reality."

"Professor —"

"I witnessed the same unfortunate pattern many times in my years of service. Otherwise promising agents infiltrating a target community and losing their objectivity, even sympathizing with the natives."

"You really are something else."

"Young lady, I —"

"Reason Two: The world has changed. It's time you accept that. In the world we live in now, respect is earned, not assumed."

I wanted to shout my full-throated support but managed to stay silent, barely.

Claire continued. "You report to me. You need to start acting like you understand that. Because what I see is an employee with an attitude problem."

"Young lady, I —"

"Agent Emerson. That's what you need to call me."

In the shocked silence that ensued, I found myself grinning ear to ear.

"Consider this an early performance review. You were given two tasks: Observe and identify. Through your ill-advised words and actions, you have diminished your capacity to carry out your mission by alienating everyone you've encountered."

"That's not —"

"No one likes you, Professor. No one trusts you. No one respects you. No one is willing to share information with you or confide in you."

"I —"

"In addition to your demonstrated inability to win the trust of your targets, you've failed to gather any helpful intel."

"That's not —"

"Name one pertinent fact, Professor. One tiny scrap of useful, actionable information."

Silence hung heavy in the air.

"You need to stop treating this mission like a vacation jaunt. This is not a return to your glory days."

More silence.

"Reason Three: You know the stakes. I'm disappointed you're not taking this more seriously. If you continue spending your time criticizing instead of listening and learning, you're of no use to me. So consider this a direct order: Stop being a jerk or I send you packing. Got it?"

After a strangled pause, the professor said, "Understood, Agent Emerson."

"Good. Task One: Start being nice to Sarah and Janie. I grew up with them. They're two of my oldest friends and wonderful people to have on your side. Try deploying some of that good old Southern courtesy you claim to value so much."

"Very well."

"The instant you see or learn something, let me know."

CHAPTER 9

I held my breath, listening as the professor shut the apartment door and Claire's boots *tap-tap-tapped* down the stairs. The instant the building's entry door opened and shut, I dashed up to my apartment and called her.

She picked up on the first ring. "Hey, Sarah, what's up?" Beneath her bright tone, I could sense the irritation she was still feeling.

From my front window, I spotted her on the sidewalk below, her long legs carrying her effortlessly toward her red sportscar.

"Have I ever told you how awesome you are?"

"Um…."

"I mean like totally, completely awesome?"

She sighed as she figured it out. "You were in the hallway."

"I happened to be, yes."

She turned around and looked up. I waved from my window.

She waved back. "You have quite a knack for, um —"

"For telling her friend how awesome she is?"

That earned me a chuckle. "Greeley is such an ass."

"I have a secret to share. I can't stand Professor Snobface. As in, I really, truly, thoroughly loathe him."

She laughed. "Promise me you won't —"

"No worries. His covert activities are safe with me."

"Thank you. But also —"

"I promise I'll keep my nose out of whatever shenanigans you and Professor Sourpuss and your secret agency whose name I'm pretending I don't know are up to."

"Thank you."

"I won't even ask what Edgar is doing here. I mean, I know what he's doing — he's spying on people. But who and why? That's what I won't ask you."

"Sarah…."

"Don't worry, my lips are sealed. Will you be at the opening reception tomorrow?"

"Count on it."

"Great. See you there."

As I watched Claire hop into her car and zoom

away, I wondered what in the world was going on. Her presence in Eagle Cove — with Edgar and the professor — confirmed my suspicions: Our tiny little flower show was definitely an espionage target.

But why? What possible reason could spies have for converging on a regional gathering of floral enthusiasts?

I shook my head, irritated. When it came to the world of espionage, my new question was merely one of a thousand I had no answer for.

Truly, my spy-related ignorance was vast and included really basic stuff, like: I didn't even know the full name of the covert agency at the heart of the recent events in Eagle Cove. I'd spent many an idle moment speculating what H.U.S.H. stood for and had come up with some fanciful possibilities, including my favorite guess:

Heroes Uniting to Save Humanity.

Catchy, right? But also laughably wrong — way too grandiose, too boastful, too movie-like, too naive, too idealistic. My recent experiences with spies had showed me that espionage was a complex, morally challenging business. As much as the folks involved might be tempted to think of themselves as heroes, my gut told me they knew their work wasn't as simple as that.

No, the name was most likely something bureaucratic. There were plenty of "U" and "S" words appropriate for a covert spy organization —

"Unified," "Strategic," "Security," and "Special" were possibilities, as was "United States." But there weren't that many spy-relevant words for "H." I could see "High" or "Hemispheric" working as the first "H," but the last "H" was most likely a noun, and that one continued to bother me.

Given that Aunt Emily's involvement went back decades, the agency's actual name probably had an old-timey feel — something self-important and clunky like "Hemispheric Unified Strategic Headquarters."

I realized I was still at the window, staring blankly at Main Street below. Basically, the things I knew about H.U.S.H. boiled down to:

One, they'd reactivated Emily because of a deep dark secret — something dangerous — that happened decades ago.

Two, their Big Bad Secret was tied to ornate metal boxes — five of them, perhaps more — retrieved a few months back from the icy depths of Heartsprings Lake.

Three, they had a secret facility on the edge of the Middlemore University campus, about a thirty-minute drive away.

Four, for reasons unknown to me, H.U.S.H. was renting my studio apartment. Using a travel agency as a front, they occasionally arranged for various unassuming guests (scientists and engineers mostly) to stay for a few days. All the visitors (except the professor) had been polite and quiet. None had caused a lick of trouble.

Five, H.U.S.H. had some good people on the payroll, including Emily, Claire, and Edgar.

Six, H.U.S.H. also employed folks who, it turned out, were really pretty awful. In the past year, two of their agents had gone on killing sprees in Eagle Cove and almost murdered me, Claire, Emily, and Matt.

And that … was pretty much it. Aside from an obvious need to improve their hiring practices, H.U.S.H. remained a black box— a mystery wrapped in an enigma hidden behind a veil of secrecy, inexplicably entwined with our small New England town.

Which made their interest in the flower show both intriguing and concerning. What were they up to?

CHAPTER 10

At last, the fateful Thursday arrived — the day of the opening reception of the Eagle Cover Flower Show. The day that Janie and I had been working toward for months. The day that Eagle Cove went kookoo gaga.

As much as I'd like to offer a thorough, detailed, reliable account of all that occurred that day, the best I can offer is a fragmentary mishmash. The sad truth is — I don't remember a lot of what happened at the opening reception of the Eagle Cove Flower Show. I'm told it's possible I never will.

Here's what I do recall. At the crack of dawn, Janie and I met at the cafe to load her minivan with equipment and supplies to bring to the reception tent — the first of multiple trips. I remember us hustling all morning to get everything set up and ready for our guests. I remember a frantic call shortly before eleven from one of our servers telling us her car wouldn't start and me racing across town to pick her up. I remember Janie giving the serving staff a detailed, informative tutorial on the menu items — the delicious sandwiches and treats inspired by English afternoon tea. I remember Mom and the mayor doing a walk-through shortly before noon and giving us a thumbs-up. And I remember the flutter of anxiety in my stomach as the first of our guests arrived at one.

I'd like to think the event would have been deemed a success had a murderer not turned it into a complete disaster. The attendees were dressed in their spring best and seemed to enjoy themselves tremendously. The serving staff did a great job keeping wine glasses topped up and trays of appetizers circulating. The mayor arrived with the judges — all three of them, miracle of miracles — and briefly took to the stage to introduce them to the crowd. I even overheard the professor pull Janie aside and tell her that her cucumber sandwiches were "surprisingly delicious." (Full credit for that pseudo-compliment goes to Claire.)

At some point I gulped down a glass of iced tea. A bit later, as you've already learned, I found the professor dead.

As for what happened after I made my horrible discovery? To this day, my recollections are fuzzy. The moments before and after that shocking event remain jumbled and distorted — a crush of images, sounds, and feelings I may never be able to place in the correct order.

When I saw the professor's blood-red eyes, I think I screamed. Or laughed? Or both?

I recall babbling a bunch of nonsense, though what I said I couldn't tell you to save my life. When no one paid me any attention, I wandered deep into the crowd, spouting even more word salad.

Finally, I managed to convince some random nice person to follow me to the dead professor to see for herself.

And from there — well, I remember a big old-fashioned hullabaloo as news of the professor's demise raced through the tent. Gasps and cries filled the air. Everyone pressed closer for a gander. The colors got brighter. The world started spinning. The reception became a kaleidoscope of swirling energy.

At a certain point I broke away from the crowd. That's when I realized I was sleepy. Gosh, so sleepy. Time for a nap!

The gorgeous, vibrant, shimmering lawn looked so soft and inviting. And so wonderfully green — such a charming color. Gratefully, I plopped down. The grass tickled my cheek but I didn't care. It smelled so good. So fresh! Wasn't spring the best?

Yes, I'd lie down to rest for a minute.

And then, just like that — I was out.

CHAPTER 11

I awoke with a splitting headache. My mouth felt dry and fuzzy.

With extreme care, I cracked an eyelid and took stock of my situation. I was lying on my side, my cheek pressed into the lawn. I had grass in my mouth. A blanket covered me.

I rolled onto my back with a groan. Above me was white canvas.

Recognition flooded in. I was in the reception tent, lying on the lawn of the Eagle Cove Common.

In the same place where I'd gone completely bonkers.

Around me I heard snores. Gingerly, I raised my head. Dozens of people were on the ground with me, covered in blankets, all of them apparently asleep.

On one side of me was Mr. Benson, dozing

peacefully. On the other, Mayor Johnson, snoring softly.

In the corner of my eye I caught movement. Doc Barnes was approaching, a bottle of water in hand.

"You're awake," he said as he knelt at my side.

I took the bottle and drank greedily. Gosh, I was thirsty. The water felt wonderful going down my throat.

"Easy now," he said, pulling the bottle from my mouth. "Small sips."

He stared at me like I was a puzzle that needed figuring out. A thin man in his fifties with a gruff manner, he wasn't one to waste time. "How do you feel?"

"Parched." My voice was scratchy. "Groggy. Fuzzy."

"To be expected. How's your vision?"

"Fine, I think?" I blinked a few times to make sure. "Maybe a bit sensitive to light?"

He leaned closer to examine my pupils.

"What in the world happened, Doc?"

He grunted. "Best we can tell, a hallucinogenic compound was added to the iced tea."

"A hallucinogen? We were *poisoned*?"

"In a word, yes. You and everyone else."

"How many of us were…?"

"Thirty-eight attendees are here sleeping it off."

"Is everyone okay?"

"Everyone will be fine. Your pupils are still dilated. You need to avoid bright light. By this time tomorrow, you should be back to normal."

"Why weren't we taken to the hospital?"

"We took several of the older attendees as a precaution. But with most of you, we decided it was best for you to sleep it off here."

"I wasn't aware that hallucinogens make one sleepy."

"They don't. It's possible the tea was double-dosed — a hallucinogen plus a narcotic. Or perhaps one beverage had the hallucinogen and another a sedative. We'll know more when the tests come back."

"The only thing I drank today was the iced tea."

"That's helpful. Narrows things down."

It was then that I remembered my awful discovery. "The professor!"

"I understand you found him."

"Did the hallucinogen kill him?"

He shook his head. "Unlikely."

My mind flashed to the professor's blood-red eyes. "Then how did…?"

"Initial examination suggests a poison causing rapid internal hemorrhaging."

"So you suspect *three* different substances were used here — a hallucinogen, a sedative, and a deadly poison?"

"That's my preliminary assessment."

A thought struck me. "Why are you telling me all of this? Usually you'd —"

"Tell you to mind your own business?"

"Yes."

He gestured toward the tent entrance. "Because the sheriff told me to."

At the mention of Matt, my heart went *thump-thump-thump*. "He's here?"

"Right outside. He's worried about you. Told me to find him the instant you woke up."

I felt it then — a wave of emotion rising from my inner depths, strong and powerful. I found myself blinking back tears.

Doc handed me a tissue — almost like he'd been expecting my reaction. "You'll feel more emotional than normal for the next day or so."

I blew my nose and let out an embarrassed laugh. "I'm sorry. I don't know what's come over me."

"The hallucinogen is what's come over you."

"So for the next day…?"

"Don't be surprised if you're more expressive than usual."

"Thanks for the warning." I blew my nose again. "So Matt really said it's okay to tell me all this?"

"He said you'd find out anyway."

That brought a laugh. Already I was feeling better. "I knew there was a reason I love him."

As soon as the dreaded word left my mouth, I gasped. It was way too early to be using that word — *waaaaaay* too early! Matt and I were taking things slowly because we were smart, experienced, responsible, serious-minded adults who knew better than to rush into anything — *right?*

What in the world was wrong with me?

"I mean…. What I mean is…."

Amused, Doc clambered to his feet and handed me the water bottle. "You're free to go. Avoid bright lights, drink lots of water — sips, not chugs — and get a good night's sleep."

I glanced at Mr. Benson still slumbering beside me. "Is it okay if I wait outside for him to wake up before heading home? I want to make sure he gets home safely."

"Of course. Shouldn't be long now."

Indeed, around me, folks were beginning to stir.

"Be careful, Sarah," Doc said as he turned to check on another patient. "Whoever did this is not someone to mess with."

Oh-so-carefully, I got to my feet and made my way past the sleeping reception attendees, each step feeling like a victory.

I emerged from the tent, shielding my eyes from the late-afternoon sun. Yellow tape cordoned off the area around the tent. Police and crime-scene technicians were everywhere, huddled in intense conversations. Beyond the tape, eager onlookers had gathered to gawk.

I'd been hoping to see Matt, but the first people I recognized were Janie and Deputy Andrea Martinez a few feet away, Janie talking and the deputy taking notes.

The instant Janie saw me, she rushed over and gave me a hug. "Sarah, thank goodness. How are you?"

"Okay, I think." I pulled back and took in my

friend's worried gaze. "How about you? Were you…?"

"I'm fine. They think it was the iced tea and I didn't have any. How are you feeling?"

"Tired but okay." Quickly, I told her what Doc Barnes had shared about the hallucinogen and sedative.

Deputy Martinez joined us. "Ms. Boone, if you're feeling up to it, I'll need a statement from you after I finish with Mrs. McKendrick."

"Of course."

Janie was staring at the tent. "A hallucinogen and a sedative? Those poor people…."

"Doc says they'll be fine," I said right away, hoping he was right.

Behind me, a familiar voice called my name. I whirled around and was engulfed in a momma bear hug. "Sarah," Mom cried. "I'm so glad you're awake."

Relief flooded through me as I saw she was okay. "No iced tea for you?"

"Not even a sip — too busy." She scanned my face anxiously. "You sure you're okay? I was so worried."

"Aside from being tired, I'm good. Doc Barnes says I'll be fit as a fiddle by tomorrow."

"How is Doris?"

"Mayor Johnson is fast asleep. Snoring, in fact.

Doc said she and the others will be waking up soon."

"That's good." She glanced around anxiously. "We need her back. Everyone is asking me to weigh in on things. *Me!*"

"I'm sure you're doing fine."

She shook her head. "I wish Emily were here. She'd know exactly how to handle this."

At the mention of Emily, I was surprised to find tears welling up. *Whoa.* Doc's warning about unexpected emotional upheaval had been totally spot-on. "I wish she could be here, too."

Deputy Martinez cleared her throat. "Mrs. McKendrick, if we could finish your statement...."

"Of course," Janie said.

As Janie and the deputy stepped away, I turned to Mom. "Okay, what do we know?"

"Nothing." Her voice rising, she added, "I mean, we know our head judge is dead. We know dozens of people are drugged and lying unconscious on the lawn of the Eagle Cove Common. We know the entire flower show is now a *crime scene.*"

"It's gonna be okay," I said quickly. "We'll get through this." I pointed to the clipboard in her hand. "Let me help you with your list."

"Yes, my list," she said, her voice returning to normal. "I need to update my list."

"Show me what you've gathered about the victims."

"Okay." She whipped out a pen. "We have most of that."

As I looked over her shoulder and scanned her list, I was completely unsurprised to find she'd already transformed the reception attendee list into a record of who had been poisoned or not, with notations for "tent," "hospital," and "OK." That was the thing about Mom: When she focused on something, she was pretty much unstoppable.

It was weird seeing my name in the "tent" category along with scads of people I knew, including Mr. Benson and Mayor Johnson.

"I can now put you in the 'OK' category," Mom said. "Right?"

"Right," I said as I continued scanning. I breathed in when I saw Polly Pence and Harriet Vale, the two other judges, also on the "tent" list. "So what happens to the flower show if the two remaining judges are … out of commission?"

"No idea," Mom said. "At this point, who knows if we'll even *have* a flower show."

Still scanning, I inhaled with alarm when I saw Gabby's friends — Mrs. Chan, Mrs. Bunch, and Ms. Hollingsworth — in the "hospital" category. "Are Gabby's gang okay?"

"I think so," she said immediately. "The paramedics took them to the hospital as a precaution due to their age. At least that's what Doc Barnes said."

"What about Gabby?"

"She's fine. Not affected at all. She insisted on going with her friends to make sure they're okay."

My eyes widened when I landed on Claire and Edgar in the "tent" category.

"Whoa — Claire? Is she okay?"

"I think so? Doc Barnes won't let me inside the tent. Medical personnel only." She looked around and lowered her voice. "You don't think what happened here is related to … you-know-what?"

She was, of course, referring to Claire's espionage activities. "I have no idea," I replied, not quite truthfully.

She looked like she wanted to press me — perhaps sensing I knew more than I was letting on — but held back when she saw Deputy Paul approaching.

His relieved gaze took me in. "Glad to see you're awake, Ms. Boone."

"Thank you."

"Nancy, they're ready and need you to…."

"Got it." Mom turned to me. "Duty calls."

"No worries. I'm fine. Deputy Martinez wants my statement. When Mr. Benson wakes up, I'll head home with him."

She pulled me in for another hug. "I want you to get a good night's sleep."

"Promise."

"Call if you need anything."

"Will do."

And then she and Deputy Paul were off to whatever important task she was needed for.

After looking around for Matt — still no sign — I called my daughter Anna and sister Grace and gave them the headline summary, which at that point was pretty basic: head judge dead, dozens of reception attendees (including me) drugged after drinking iced tea laced with a hallucinogen and a sedative. I told them I was exhausted but otherwise okay. I assured them I'd be back to normal after a good night's sleep. I also told them Mom was fine — no iced tea for her — and extremely busy dealing with everything.

By the time I'd finished updating them, Deputy Martinez was done with Janie and ready for me. Calmly and methodically, she took me through my day.

Or at least she tried to. Very quickly, it became apparent to both of us that there was a lot I didn't remember. What little I recalled seemed jumbled up.

"I'm sorry," I told her. "Everything's so fuzzy."

"What you're experiencing is common. More will come later."

"I wish I could remember something that would be of help."

"Give it time."

I glanced around. "So … where's Matt?"

"On a call with the governor's office. He'll be back soon."

I gulped. *The governor's office?* For the first time, it dawned on me that the impact of today's events would extend well beyond Eagle Cove.

Deputy Martinez gestured to the reception tent. "Other attendees are starting to wake up. I have to gather more statements."

"Of course."

"We can meet tomorrow to complete yours."

"Sounds good."

And then I saw him. Striding with purpose and determination to the crime scene, his handsome face tense, his worried eyes scanning the crowd until he locked onto —

Me.

CHAPTER 13

Matt slipped under the crime scene tape, ran up to me, and swept me into his arms.

"Sarah," he whispered in my ear. "You're okay."

"I'm fine," I whispered back. Tears came as I gripped him tightly, fiercely, never wanting the hug to end.

He pulled back to examine my face, his eyes filled with relief. "Let's go somewhere more private." With his arm around my waist, he led me around the corner of the reception tent to a spot where a million people weren't rushing to and fro.

And then he kissed me. Oh my, he kissed me. I'll freely admit I melted into him completely and totally and not just because the hallucinogen swirling through my bloodstream had released my inhibitions. Everything I'd always felt for him came welling up in a huge rush.

When we finally surfaced for air, the moment seemed to go on as we just looked at each other. Have I mentioned before how attractive he is, with his broad shoulders and thick brown hair? I found myself zooming in on the stubble on his strong jaw, on the warmth of his deep brown eyes, on his gorgeous lashes — way longer and thicker than mine, which was totally not fair — all while breathing in the wonderful scent of him.

He brushed a strand of hair from my cheek. "What am I going to do with you, Sarah Boone?"

"Exactly this," I murmured. "Exactly what you're doing right now."

"I am *not* a fan of finding you unconscious. Second time in six months. Two times too many."

The first time, of course, had been the previous fall, when an assassin knocked me out with a dart full of horse tranquilizer.

"Well," I said, leaning into him, "if it makes you feel better, I agree completely. Being rendered unconscious is not my idea of fun."

He raised my chin and kissed me again. "I'm so relieved you're okay."

"Me, too." I swallowed. "Now, about the professor...."

A smile came to his lips. "I was wondering how long that would take. What about him?"

"I assume he was murdered?"

"Your assumption is correct."

"Doc Barnes suspects poison."

"Starting to feel like your usual inquisitive self, I see."

"Maybe I find mysteries invigorating. Any idea who did it?"

"Too early to know. We haven't even begun processing the scene."

"Because Doc Barnes is using the tent to treat people?"

He nodded. "Medical takes priority."

"You can start by interviewing me. And I'll state up front — I had motive."

He smiled. "Oh, is that so?"

"Couldn't stand the man. Professor Greeley was the rudest, most arrogant human being I've ever met."

He pulled me in for another hug, his strong arms feeling wonderful. "What can I do to persuade you to stay out of this?"

"Well," I said, finding comfort in the steady beating of his heart. "The way I see it, I'm pretty much your Number One suspect."

"Mmm, is that so?"

"I mean, look at the facts."

"Walk me through your case."

"Point one. Motive. As already disclosed, I couldn't stand the guy."

"Duly noted."

"Point two. Opportunity. I was the one who discovered the body. I was at the scene of the crime the entire time."

"Can't argue with that."

"Point three. Means. It probably would have been easy-peasy for me to get my hands on the poison, whatever it was, and put it into Professor Sourpuss's teacup."

"You make a compelling case." He sighed and pulled back to look me in the eye. "Since that's the way you're playing it, here's a formal question, sheriff to potential suspect. Did you kill him?"

I gazed up at him. "I solemnly swear I did not."

"Then I hereby clear you as a person of interest."

"Thank you."

"And absolve you of any need to get involved."

"Well," I said, wrapping my arms around him again. "A bunch of my friends were on the scene, too."

He sighed. "Sarah…."

"Professor Snobface was mean to everyone. Insults were a way of life for him."

"You can't be thinking…."

"I'm not saying anyone we know is the culprit. But until the killer is found, everyone at the reception is under a cloud of suspicion."

As the words left my mouth, a thought came and I tensed.

Matt must have felt it. "What is it you want to tell me?"

I didn't have a choice, I realized — I hoped Claire wouldn't be upset. "I saw the professor and Claire together yesterday afternoon. They were having a private chat in the studio apartment."

He let out a sigh. He knew Claire worked for a secret government agency and understood what "private chat" meant. "Which I suppose you ... accidentally overheard?"

"Something like that."

"What did you accidentally overhear?"

"The professor was here on an assignment. To 'observe and identify.'"

"Observe what?"

"The flower show, I think."

"And identify what or whom?"

"Not a clue."

"What else did they talk about?"

"Mostly she laid into him for being so rude to everyone. Told him to shape up or ship out."

"I'll ask her when she wakes up."

"Yes, please do. She wouldn't tell me who or what he was supposed to identify." After a pause, I added, "By the way, she has a colleague here. He may know stuff, too."

He sighed. "A colleague?"

"His name is Edgar. He's working as the flower show's videographer."

"Of course he is. And you know that because…?"

"The day I went to Middlemore back in February, to that building that's really a spy center? He was one of the security guards there."

"You're saying he's not really a security guard. Or a videographer."

"I'm pretty sure he's an agent like Claire."

He grunted. "Her agency's involvement is the last thing I need. Any guesses who or what they're after?"

"Honestly, not a clue. Last time they showed up, it was about those metal boxes hidden in the lake."

"Speaking of, has Claire shared anything more about them — what they are, what they're for?"

"Not a peep. Which is very annoying."

At that moment, Deputy Paul peeked his head around the corner of the tent. "Sheriff, they're waiting for you in the main tent."

Matt sighed. "Gotta go."

I disengaged reluctantly. "I assume you have a very busy evening ahead of you?"

"You assume right."

"As soon as Mr. Benson wakes up, I'll be heading home with him."

He looked at me intently, his brown eyes alive with concern. "You sure you're okay?"

"A good night's sleep and all will be good."

"I'll call you in the morning."

CHAPTER 14

Mr. Benson woke up a short while later and, after Doc Barnes checked him out, the two of us left the Common and walked home. After getting him settled in his apartment and calling Gabby to check in with her — she was camped out for the night at the hospital with her gang, refusing to budge from their bedsides, even though all of them were apparently doing fine — I went upstairs and promptly crashed.

I awoke the next morning feeling stiff and sluggish. Beneath my comfy comforter, I carefully took stock, stretching this way and that to make sure my limbs were operating as usual. Then I sat up and blinked a bunch of times, focusing on different things before finally sighing with relief. As predicted, the drugs I'd ingested had apparently worked their way through my system.

I swung my legs out of bed and stood up, readying myself for whatever was in store. One didn't need to be a psychic to know the day would be a doozy. By any measure, Eagle Cove was in a heap of trouble. A man murdered, dozens drugged, a flower show in upheaval — where to begin?

I gasped when I saw the bedside clock. It was nearly nine. I'd slept for *thirteen hours*. With a mixture of dread and curiosity, I grabbed my phone and scrolled through the avalanche of texts awaiting me.

The messages from Matt held no surprises. The cafe would need to stay closed until crime scene technicians and health inspectors examined the kitchen for traces of the drugs added to the iced tea. "They should finish up this afternoon," he added. "Sorry."

He also told me his team had searched the studio apartment and that the studio needed to remain off-limits until the professor's belongings were removed.

Mom's texts were, as usual, to the point. "Call me when you wake up. I need to know you're okay!" Followed by: "The mayor and I will be at the cafe at 10. Get dressed!"

Janie had texted to tell me she'd come to the cafe to let in the health inspectors when they were ready.

Anna, Grace, and Claire had all pinged to see how I was doing.

With a sigh, I stood up and began the process of making myself presentable to the world.

Forty-five minutes later, clad in sensible jeans, sneakers, and a favorite blue sweater, I went down a flight and knocked on Mr. Benson's door. He answered in his bathrobe and, after assuring me he was feeling tired but otherwise fine, told me Gabby had called from the hospital to report that her friends were all doing well.

Relieved, I went downstairs and let myself into the cafe. For the first morning in months, the place wasn't filled with the wonderful aroma of Janie's muffins and the hubbub of happy customers. With a fierce pang of longing, I realized how much I loved this little place.

In the mail slot in the front door was the morning edition of the *Eagle Cove Gazette.* I hurried over and gasped when I opened the front page. The headlines couldn't have been more dramatic:

CHAOS AND DEATH AT THE EAGLE COVE FLOWER SHOW

HEAD JUDGE POISONED

DOZENS DOSED WITH POWERFUL HALLUCINOGEN

Seeing the truth laid out so dramatically was

jarring. The lead article, bylined by Wendy Travers, was uncomfortably detailed. I frowned when I read:

> *Greeley's body was discovered by Sarah Boone, the event caterer and co-owner of Emily's Eats cafe in downtown Eagle Cove.*
>
> *Upon finding the body, Boone reportedly exclaimed, "Hey ho, hey ho, lookie lookie dookie dookie, the little egg man is dead." She then curled up on the lawn and fell asleep.*
>
> *Boone, who has been involved in multiple homicide events since moving to Eagle Cove last fall, was among those who drank the iced tea suspected of being laced with a hallucinogen and a sedative. Boone and her cafe partner, Janie McKendrick, prepared and served the iced tea to reception attendees.*

Grrrrr. Even if the reporting was accurate — and it probably was, I was willing to concede — had Wendy really needed to share all those details? I mean, in what way was *lookie lookie dookie dookie* relevant to anything? Why the need to hammer home the cafe's connection to the hallucinogenic iced tea? And what possible significance did the previous homicides have to the flower show?

I set down the paper. There was a connection, I realized. All of the murders were tied to H.U.S.H.

Or might be, I amended. We didn't know yet

who'd killed the professor or why. Espionage was the likely reason but not the only one. I'd need to keep an open mind.

I was still at the counter, lost in thought, when a knock came from the cafe's front door.

It was Mayor Johnson. I hurried over to let her in. She marched past me, the *Gazette* clenched in her hand, her face a case study in anger-fueled determination.

Uh oh. Even on her sunny days, the mayor was a formidable presence. When she got like this, I did my best to steer clear.

"Mayor Johnson," I said cautiously. "How are you feeling?"

"Sarah, have you seen Wendy Travers?"

"Sorry, no."

Her grip on the newspaper tightened, the crinkling echoing in the empty cafe. "I was told she's headed here."

"She hasn't arrived yet. You're welcome to wait. How are you feeling?"

She sighed. "Physically and mentally, extremely tired. Your mother and I were up most of the night. Doc Barnes warned me I'd be more emotional than usual and he was right, which is making today even more of a challenge."

"What's the latest from the Common?"

"The two main competition tents have been cleared for use, but the reception tent remains a crime scene. The sheriff may release it back to us this afternoon."

After a deep breath, I asked the question I'd been wondering all morning. "What about the flower show?"

The mayor squared her shoulders. "The show will go on."

Relief flooded through me — I'd been hoping for that. "I'm glad to hear."

"We made the call last night after a careful assessment of the health, safety, and operational concerns."

It was odd hearing a flower show — which on the surface was just a bunch of plants being brought to a place to be enjoyed by a bunch of people — described as an event with security and operational concerns. Yet that's exactly what it was. And it was up to the mayor, sheriff, and event planners to figure out how to respond to what could only be described as a catastrophe.

The newspaper in the mayor's hand crinkled again. "The *Gazette* story is getting wide coverage. Press inquiries are flooding in. All the nearby TV stations have dispatched news teams. The national networks have taken notice."

"Oh, dear."

The mayor shook her head. "By lunchtime, this town will be a circus."

"And it's your job to contain the damage."

She nodded grimly. "Which is why I need to find Wendy."

"The other reporters have read her story, which means they'll be asking for her help with local knowledge...."

"Which means it's important that she understand important facts about the situation and how we're moving forward."

I had to admit — I was impressed. In the midst of disaster and despite not feeling her best, the mayor was working hard to shape the narrative and protect the town's interests from the imminent media onslaught.

"Mom texted earlier. She said she'd be with you."

"She's setting up a media center on the Common."

"A media center? What does that involve?"

The mayor shrugged. "It's not complicated. A tent with chairs, tables, power, wifi, and endless coffee. Journalists are simple creatures." She glanced toward the kitchen. "Though I'm wondering...."

"Sorry, we can't provide treats today," I said right away. "Matt and the health inspector need to look at the kitchen before we can reopen."

"Perhaps tomorrow?"

"I'll let you know."

She regarded me for a moment. "About what I said yesterday. I want to apologize for my manner."

"Oh, no need."

"I hope I didn't upset you."

"You didn't. Not at all."

"I meant what I said, or at least what I remember saying. Every single word. I'm very glad you moved back to Eagle Cove and I'm thrilled you and Janie reopened the cafe. But I'm also concerned about your curious nature. I hope I don't have to remind you how important it is for you to stay out of this investigation."

"Mayor Johnson, I —"

The newspaper crinkled again. "The *Gazette* put a target on your back. Every reporter coming to Eagle Cove will want to interview you."

My stomach sank. I hadn't considered that. "I have no interest in being part of the story."

"Let me know if you run into problems."

As if on cue, a figure appeared outside the cafe window — Wendy Travers, the *Gazette*'s ace reporter. When she saw us, she eagerly stepped inside.

"Good morning, Wendy," I heard myself say politely. Apparently, without being aware of it, I'd decided to not confront her about her excessively detailed article, or at least not yet.

Wendy took us in, her gaze calculating and cool. Several years younger and ten pounds slimmer than me, she was an attractive woman with sharp brown eyes and shoulder-length brown hair. From experience, I knew she was nobody's pushover. "Sarah, Mayor Johnson, I'd like to speak with you about the mass poisoning at the flower show."

"Before we get to that," the mayor said, "I'd like to discuss the language the *Gazette* used to describe the events that occurred."

Wendy pointed to the paper in the mayor's hand. "'Chaos' and 'death' are quite accurate."

The mayor shook her head. "The words are inadequate and, as a result, misleading. They fail to provide a complete understanding of what is happening here."

Wendy's back stiffened. "Every word in my story is accurate."

"I'm more concerned about what *isn't* in your story."

"Like what?"

"Like the fact that Eagle Cove responded swiftly and effectively to an unprecedented event. Medical professionals successfully triaged treatment at the scene for more than forty people. Moments ago, the hospital announced that the five people admitted overnight as a precaution are all doing well and will be released today."

Wendy was scribbling in her notebook. The mayor had shared fresh news. "What about the investigation? I've been told that Professor Greeley's death is being treated as a homicide."

"What I can tell you is that the investigation is active and proceeding rapidly. The flower show's two main tents have been cleared for use. The reception tent will remain off-limits until the scene is fully processed. The sheriff is holding a press conference at one to provide a full update."

"At one? Where?"

"We're setting up a media tent on the Common with free wifi and coffee."

Wendy looked up from her notebook. "You've got to give me more than that."

"So do you," the mayor shot back. "The *Gazette* needs to report — accurately, thoroughly, even-handedly — the facts about Eagle Cove's successful and effective response."

Wendy frowned. "The headlines and focus are up to Bob," she said, referring to Bob Underhill, the owner and publisher of the *Gazette*.

"I've already spoken with him. He told me his stories are a reflection of the best efforts of his talented reporting team."

Wendy's frown deepened. "You're saying I've been unfair."

"No, I am not. We all had a busy night. You had a lot to report. What I'm asking is that you make every effort to be thorough and complete in your reporting. As a serious journalist, I know you won't be swayed by the lure of dramatic, sensationalist coverage. The town's response to these terrible events is an essential part of the story."

After a long, skeptical pause, Wendy let out a sigh. "Fine."

"Thank you. Now, about what's coming. I know your media colleagues are reaching out to you for your help. As you respond, keep in mind how important the *Gazette* is to Eagle Cove. All of us are relying on you and Bob to cover these events responsibly, fairly, and accurately."

"You still haven't told me what's in it for me."

"We'd like to offer you the opportunity to 'embed' with me and Nancy this weekend."

Wendy's eyes widened. "Meaning?"

"You're with us all day. No limitations. All we ask is that you report accurately and completely."

"Who else gets this special access?"

"No one. *Gazette* only."

Though Wendy's expression remained skeptical, her shoulders tensed with interest.

"Deal," she said.

"Good. Let's head to the town office. There's a lot to do."

As I watched their negotiation unfold, I had to admit I admired how the two of them had handled themselves. The discussion could have turned heated, but instead they'd reached an agreement that gave both of them what they wanted. Wendy would get exclusive behind-the-scenes access and the mayor would get the opportunity to show Wendy everything the town was doing to respond to the crisis.

Wendy swiveled toward me. "Before we head out, a few questions for you, Sarah."

I tensed. "I don't have anything to say."

"Why does every murder in Eagle Cove involve you?"

My cheeks flamed red. *Why indeed?* "I have no idea."

"Every time the season changes, you find bodies. Autumn comes, dead bodies. Winter comes, more dead bodies. Now it's spring."

"Wendy...."

She sidled closer, her tone inviting. "We've talked about this before. Come on. Tell me what's really going on."

As I've said before, our local reporter was no dummy. She knew there was a story behind the story — a secret narrative swirling beneath the surface of our small town — and she suspected I knew a lot about it.

"I gave my statement to the sheriff's team."

"That's not what I'm talking about and you know it."

Fortunately, my phone chose that moment to buzz. I pulled it out and saw it was Matt.

"Sorry," I said, trying to sound regretful. "I have to get this. Can we talk later?"

Wendy frowned when she realized I wasn't giving her a choice. "I'll find you."

"Thanks."

As the mayor hustled Wendy out of the cafe, I brought the phone to my ear. "Hey."

"Sarah," Matt said, his voice low and rumbly. "How are you feeling?"

"Fine. Tired but otherwise okay. How about you?"

"Same."

"I got your texts. No worries. The cafe is closed and the studio apartment is locked up tight."

"Thanks."

I could tell from his voice how exhausted he was. "Did you work through the night?"

"Had to."

"Have you slept?"

"I'll sleep tonight."

"That's not good."

"I'll get shut-eye later — promise."

"Anything I can help with?"

"Actually, there is," he said. "I need your help. Can you come to the crime scene right away?"

CHAPTER 15

My heart jumped. "Of course," I said immediately. "See you in a few."

After a quick glance around the cafe to make sure all was good, I texted Janie to let her know I'd been summoned by Matt. Then I headed out.

When I reached the Common a few moments later, the first thing I saw was the yellow tape surrounding the reception tent.

Deputy Paul was standing guard. "The sheriff's inside."

"Thank you, Deputy," I replied, slipping under the tape.

The inside of the tent looked pretty much like it had yesterday afternoon, minus the dozens of drugged reception attendees slumbering on the lawn. The tables, chairs, and flower displays were all as they had been.

Matt was at the judges' table, listening to his phone. He waved me over.

"Call as soon as you know," he said into the phone, then slipped it into his pocket and pulled me in for a long hug. "How are you?"

"Good," I said, enjoying how he allowed the moment to linger. "Much better."

"I'm glad."

He stepped back and gazed at me with relief.

"So," I said, trying to ignore a rush of feelings that included pleasure and affection and so much more. "You said you needed my help."

"Right." He stepped back, then glanced around as if trying to decide where to start. "The state lab has identified the hallucinogen found in the iced tea."

"That was fast."

"The case is high-profile. They're fast-tracking our tests."

"What did they find? LSD? Mushrooms?"

He pointed to a nearby table. "Not quite."

On the table was an array of equipment that looked like it belonged to the crime-scene techs, along with a single potted plant — a pretty orchid whose bright yellow petals were accented with small brown spots.

I frowned. "Wait. You're talking about the orchid?"

He pulled out his notebook and read from it.

"*Trichocentrum cebolleta*. Originally from Central and South America, now cultivated by orchid enthusiasts worldwide. This particular specimen is from the main tent. It was entered into competition by Donald Benson."

"This is *Mr. Benson's* orchid?"

"It turns out this particular species of orchid contains entheogens, which are" — again he consulted his notes — "psychoactive substances that cause changes in perception, mood, and behavior."

"You're saying an *orchid* got me high?"

"Yes."

"Talk about flower power."

"I was on the phone this morning with experts getting a crash course in plant-based hallucinogens. Apparently, many plants — including mushrooms, as you said — have psychoactive properties."

"Shrooms were big in college."

"Still are. This particular orchid's entheogens are believed to be similar to those found in peyote."

"Remind me — peyote's a cactus?"

"A cactus indigenous to northern Mexico and the American Southwest, used for thousands of years in religious ceremonies to reduce inhibitions and induce euphoria."

I thought about Mr. Benson and his hula dance. "You're saying this cute little orchid is a floral version of peyote."

He shrugged. "The experts I talked with said

psychoactive plants haven't been well-studied —
that when it comes to the science of them, there's a
great deal we don't know. But everyone I spoke with
said the effects are real. The plants have been used
for a variety of medicinal and religious purposes
throughout human history."

"Do the symptoms include hallucinations?"

"Was that what you experienced?"

"Well...." I thought for a moment about how
to describe what I'd gone through. "I felt
euphoric, upbeat, happy. My visual experience
changed as well. The colors seemed brighter, more
vibrant."

"Any lingering effects?"

"No, pretty much back to normal." I gestured to
the orchid. "You said this plant is Mr. Benson's.
Surely you don't believe...."

He shook his head. "The amount of
hallucinogen required to dose dozens of people is
far greater than what's found in a single plant. Also,
the leaves need to be ground up. This plant is fully
intact, which means Donald's orchid isn't the
source."

"I spoke with him a short while ago. He's
recovering well."

"Good. I need to talk with him. He knows a lot
about orchids and the orchid community."

"You're looking for someone with expert
knowledge."

He shrugged. "I know what you're thinking. Flower experts at a flower show."

"Hundreds of 'em. All here. You've got your work cut out for you."

"I'm hoping Donald can point us in the right direction."

"Have you been able to narrow the list of suspects based on access to the reception?"

"Unfortunately, no."

I frowned, not following. "But the reception was ticketed. The only people allowed in the tent were invited guests."

He walked to a side of the tent and pushed at the canvas, revealing a three-foot slit. "Someone cut through the side."

I inhaled sharply. "Anyone could have slipped in and out."

"Which means it's possible the killer wasn't invited to the reception."

"Or the killer sliced the canvas to lead us to believe he wasn't invited."

"Yep."

The magnitude of the investigative challenge began to sink in. Again I saw how tired he was. "You're going to figure this out. I know you will."

"Thanks."

"So…. Doc Barnes said a sedative was added as well?"

"Nothing exotic there. Garden-variety sleeping pills. Widely prescribed."

"And the drugs were added to the iced tea?"

"Yes, the orchid extract and the sleeping pills were both in the iced tea."

"We prepared the iced tea yesterday morning here at the tent."

"Janie told us."

I thought back to the rush and bustle of the event. "It would have been easy for someone to add the drugs when no one was looking."

"Yep," he said. "Pretty much anyone could have done it."

"Dosing the iced tea seems so … indiscriminate. The killer didn't care who might get hurt."

"Our working theory is that the killer's goal was to impede the investigation."

I sighed. "Hate to say it, but doing that was kind of brilliant. With so many people drugged, you had a medical crisis to deal with first."

"And now we have dozens of witnesses whose recollections were compromised by a hallucinogenic compound."

"So in terms of opportunity, what you're saying is that pretty much anyone in Eagle Cove with flower expertise could have done this."

"I wish I could narrow it to that, but no," he said with a sigh. "Flower expertise wasn't essential.

The killer could have acquired the orchid extract from any number of orchid growers."

Yeesh. "So what you're saying is that literally *anyone* at or near the flower show yesterday afternoon could have done this."

"Pretty much."

"I assume the working theory is that whoever drugged the iced tea also killed the professor?"

"That's the working theory, yes."

"So how did the professor die?"

"His tea was dosed with a type of plant alkaloid. The lab's working to narrow down which one. Within minutes of drinking the poisoned tea, his body went into toxic shock."

I shuddered. "That's fast. What exactly is an alkaloid?"

He looked to his notebook. "Alkaloids are a class of organic compounds containing nitrogen that are produced by plants, fungi, bacteria, and animals. Many have beneficial medical uses, but some are highly toxic. Among the poisonous plant alkaloids are strychnine and belladonna, also known as deadly nightshade."

"Oh, gosh," I exclaimed. "Lots of classic mystery novels use either deadly nightshade or strychnine as the murder weapon. That makes this murder part of a grand tradition."

He raised an eyebrow. "A grand tradition?"

"Okay," I said, backtracking. "Not *grand*, I guess. And hopefully not a tradition."

He smiled. Despite his exhaustion, he was enjoying having me here.

"One more thing," I said, eager to take advantage of his willingness to share. "I've always wanted to know — what does 'toxic shock' actually mean?"

He shrugged. "Different things, depending on the toxin. Some toxins interfere with breathing and muscle movement, causing victims to basically suffocate to death. Other toxins interrupt the heart's electrical signals and result in heart attacks. Still others induce internal bleeding and strokes. Basically, through one biological mechanism or another, the body shuts down."

I shuddered as I contemplated Professor Greeley's final moments. "Did he cry out for help? Would he have known he was in trouble?"

"If he did, no one noticed. The poison may have interfered with his consciousness, speech, or movement. We'll know more when the autopsy and toxicology tests are complete."

"And you said the specific alkaloid hasn't been identified yet?"

"Not yet."

"He was sitting when I found him. Why didn't he fall out of his chair?"

"His body position was well-balanced. Any

convulsions he had weren't enough to dislodge him."

"And his blood-red eyes?"

"Internal hemorrhage."

I shuddered again. "It's all so terrible. One minute you're alive, full of venom and spite. And the next...."

Matt's expression was grim. "Full of poison — and dead."

"The poison was definitely in his teacup?"

"And the teapot. The lab found residue in both."

I remembered something. "He demanded his own pot of tea."

"Janie told us. She prepared it for him."

"Oh, my."

"Don't share that, by the way. We're not releasing details about the teapot, at least not today."

"Got it. What details are you releasing?"

He let out a sigh. "I told the *Gazette* that Greeley's death is being investigated as a homicide."

"And the manner of death?"

"A type of plant alkaloid."

"You're sharing that detail because...?"

"We're hoping it shakes things loose."

I nodded. Tapping the expertise of those in town for the show made sense.

"As for how the poison was delivered, I assume it was dissolved in the hot tea?"

"That's what we believe, yes."

"Could the poison have been placed in the pot *before* the tea was prepared?"

"Yes."

"Or infused into the tea leaves?"

"Possibly."

"Did he like milk or sugar in his tea?"

"Sugar. And yes, that's being analyzed as well."

I shook my head with dismay. "There are so many possibilities. The poison could have been in the tea leaves, the pot, the cup, or the sugar. You have to find out who had access to any and all of them, both before and after Janie prepared the tea."

"That's right."

"The killer isn't making this easy for you."

"Not at all."

"At least you have an idea of *how* he was killed. What about the *when*?"

"We know Janie brought the pot of tea to the professor shortly after he arrived at the reception at one-thirty. You found him dead at about two. If the poison was added after Janie brought him the tea, then we have our window."

I frowned as I thought it through. "The killer could have seen the teapot next to the professor and known with a fair amount of certainty that the professor would be the person drinking from it."

"That's one of the reasons I asked you to come here. Think back. What do you recall about that half hour? Do you remember where the professor was? Who he was talking with?"

"Oh, gosh." I glanced around the tent, suddenly anxious. "I was so busy and there were so many people here and that's when I started feeling the effects of the drugs...."

"Honestly, I'm not expecting you to remember anything relevant. But let's give it a shot, okay?"

I took a deep breath and tried to focus. Even before the hallucinogen began playing with my perceptions and emotions, the event had been a blurred, frenetic rush.

"It's mostly just snippets," I said after a moment. "Flashes. All jumbled up. When I spoke with Mayor Johnson, I remember thinking she was acting a bit...."

"Out of character?"

"Yes. I saw Mr. Benson joking with Janie and doing a hula dance."

His eyebrows rose. "Donald was doing the hula?"

"Crazy, right? Then I noticed the professor asleep at the judges' table and thought, 'The day's too lovely to let him be grouchy and alone,' so I went over and...."

As I remembered the professor's blood-filled eyes, my chest tightened. Immediately, I chastised myself. I'd loathed the man — why was I getting worked up?

Matt's voice exuded patience. "It's okay. Take your time."

With difficulty, I pushed back the unwanted emotions. "I'm a terrible witness. I'm sorry."

"Nothing to be sorry about. You were dosed with two powerful drugs. Do you remember anything else about the teapot?"

I thought for a moment. "Sorry, no."

"How about the sliced canvas in the side of the tent? Anything come to mind?"

I shook my head.

He took me through the statement I'd given Deputy Martinez the previous afternoon, both of us hoping that a useful memory might surface from my drug-addled brain.

"I'm sorry," I finally said.

"It's okay. Sometimes memories come back, sometimes they don't."

"I'll let you know the instant I remember anything new."

His phone buzzed. He looked at it and grimaced. "Sorry, gotta go. I'm expected at the station."

"No worries. Give me a call when you can."

He took my hands in his. "There's one more thing you can do."

"Name it."

His expression was dead-serious. "I want you to be careful. We're up against a bold, clever, resourceful killer, someone who's comfortable with risk and smart enough to commit a crime without leaving evidence tying the crime back to him or her."

I gulped as a frisson of fear shot through me.

His next words were even more sobering. "This was also the act of a desperate individual. The murder was committed in public. The killer didn't care about collateral damage. There's no telling what he or she might do next."

CHAPTER 16

It was only as Matt strode away that his words fully sank in. I shivered. He was completely right — the killer was audacious, daring, skillful, and ruthless. And though the investigation was moving forward quickly, the evidence so far was leading only to new questions.

I left the reception tent. As the sun warmed my cheeks, my mood began to lift. Around me on the Common, flower enthusiasts were flocking to the big white tents, the canvas crisp and fresh against the green of the lawn and the blue of the sky. A soft breeze carried a floral scent, beckoning me closer.

The flower show was a very good thing and I was glad it was moving forward. Flowers were more than pretty plants — they were wonders of nature, providers of comfort, and holders of memories.

They were with us during many of life's most important moments.

Out of habit, I glanced at my watch. For the first time in months, it was a Friday morning and I had absolutely nothing to do. The cafe was shut down and would remain so until the investigators inspected the kitchen. The reception tent was still a crime scene, which meant I couldn't do cleanup there.

The thought came: I could find Mom and give her a hand. She was juggling a million balls — she'd welcome the extra help.

Buoyed by my new goal, I headed for the competition tents and quickly found myself surrounded by flowers of all sorts — peonies and roses, orchids and hydrangeas, tiger lilies and dahlias, lilacs and gardenias and so many more. Under the glow of the white canvas, the space seemed to be bursting with life. Along the sides of the tent were the gorgeous flower arrangements entered into the show. Each arrangement stood on a pedestal of its own and offered something different and exciting. In the center of the tent, lined up prettily on rows of long tables, were the individual potted plants competing in the various horticulture categories (Best Orchid, Best Dahlia, and so on).

Despite my goal of quickly finding Mom, I found myself slowing down, captivated by the beauty of the lovely flowers around me. I've always loved flowers, but seeing them gathered together like this — in this joyous explosion of colors, shapes, and scents — was truly dazzling.

The crowd around me seemed equally enthused. Clearly yesterday's chaos hadn't kept folks away. If anything, based on the tidbits of conversation I overheard, the professor's death and the mass hallucinogenic trip were prime topics of conversation. The comments ran the gamut and included:

"I heard his eyes were blood-red — like a rabid wolf."

"Can you imagine? All those people, dressed to the nines for a proper English tea, stoned out of their gourds?"

"I spoke with her this morning — she's fine. She said the experience reminded her of that weekend at the lake. Yeah, *that* weekend."

"Obviously whoever did it is a complete and total maniac."

Through the crowd, I saw Mr. Benson escorting our two remaining judges, Polly and Harriet. The judges were holding clipboards and pens and carefully examining the competition entries.

Mr. Benson smiled as I approached. "Sarah, how are you feeling?"

"Good, thanks. I was about to ask you the same."

"Much improved." He gestured toward Polly

and Harriet. "Have you met our esteemed judges? I'm volunteering as their guide for the day."

"Yes, we've been introduced." I turned to them. "I saw your names on the list of those who were sleeping in the tent yesterday afternoon. How are you feeling?"

"Much better," Harriet said. "I slept well last night, which helped. Yesterday was rather difficult."

"Yes, a good night's sleep helped," Polly said. "I'm not unfamiliar with the effects we experienced. What upsets me is the unwitting nature of what occurred."

"You mean," I said, wanting to make sure I was following, "someone getting you high without your consent?"

"That's the heart of it. What I choose to consume is for me to decide and no one else."

"Totally agree. I assume you're doing the judging right now?"

"Yes," Polly said. "We're a bit behind schedule, so...."

"Of course." I stepped back and watched with interest as they examined each entry, occasionally scribbling notes next to what looked like a list of numbers.

Harriet bent closer to a small orange lily in a garishly painted pot — Gabby's pot, I realized.

"A lovely specimen," Harriet said as she nudged

the stem with her pen. "Though the pot does it no favors."

Polly added, "That is what one calls a *statement*."

"Does the pot matter?" I asked.

"Presentation matters," Harriet said promptly.

"So if the pot distracts…."

"Then yes, it's a factor," Polly confirmed.

Mr. Benson had been listening uncomfortably. "Perhaps I can provide some context. The pot is owned by a good friend of mine. She has a colorful personality and likes things that reflect her boldness and vivacity. She received the pot as a gift from a dear friend who passed away last year."

The two judges were listening politely.

"I believe she chose this particular pot as a way to honor our friend, who for many years was head of the flower show's organizing committee."

"Thank you for explaining, Donald," Polly said gently. "The story behind an entry can be very helpful when it comes to judging."

Polly's words, I realized, were intended to smooth over the awkwardness of the moment. From the relief on Mr. Benson's face, it looked like they'd succeeded.

"We haven't asked you yet, Sarah," Harriet said. "How are you feeling?"

"Mostly fine," I replied. "I slept for thirteen hours last night."

"My goodness."

"I know, right? I can't tell you the last time I did that." Before my nerves deserted me, I added, "About what happened yesterday. I wanted to offer both of you my condolences for the loss of the professor."

The two women went still. Mr. Benson shot me a sharp glance.

"I mean," I continued, "I figured you knew him from judging other flower shows, but maybe I got that wrong?"

The two women looked at each other, silent. Then Harriet cleared her throat. "Yes, we knew Beauregard. We'll remember him for who he was."

I kept a sympathetic expression on my face as I absorbed what she was really saying: *We didn't like him and we won't miss him.*

Then I said, "Any idea who might have wanted to kill him?"

Polly blinked. "Kill him?"

"Apparently it was murder."

"Murder?" she repeated. "I assumed he died from a reaction to the drugs we all ingested."

"The *Gazette* is reporting foul play. Given how the professor looked when I found him, I can't say I'm surprised."

"What do you mean?"

"His eyes were blood-red."

Polly gasped and Harriet breathed in sharply.

"The drugs in the iced tea couldn't have caused that, apparently. So I'm guessing he died from something different. Something only he was exposed to."

"How awful," Harriet said.

"Do the authorities know what caused the hemorrhage?" Polly whispered.

"I don't know."

"This is a terrible business," Harriet said. "Simply terrible."

"Listen, I'm sorry I brought it up. Everyone here is so relieved you agreed to stay on and continue judging our little flower show."

"We almost didn't agree," Harriet said. "Your sheriff and mayor are quite persuasive."

Polly was trembling. "Harriet, maybe we should leave. What if we're next?"

"Polly," Harriet said, clearly distressed by her friend's fear. "I understand your concern, but we need to hold steady. There is nothing here to suggest that judges are being targeted. The police have no evidence of anything of the sort."

"But...."

"We told the mayor we'd see this through. I can't imagine the sheriff would be happy about us scurrying away. We'll be done in two days. We'll leave then."

"But what if…?"

"Polly," Harriet said firmly, "there's nothing to worry about. I promise you. Everything is going to be fine."

CHAPTER 17

And that seemed to be the end of it. Reluctantly, Polly followed Harriet's lead and returned her attention to the flowers.

As I watched them poke and prod the contest entries, occasionally taking notes and quietly conferring with each other, I rewound our conversation.

Their careful answer about Professor Greeley confirmed what Mom had already shared: They hadn't liked the professor and weren't going to miss him.

Their surprise at learning he'd been murdered was also interesting. Was their ignorance believable? Everyone else in town seemed to know already — or at least assume — that the professor's death was intentional.

Of course, I immediately reminded myself, Polly

and Harriet weren't locals, which meant they lacked access to the instantaneous and comprehensive information superhighway known as the Eagle Cove gossip network. They'd also spent most of the past twenty-four hours either high or asleep. So not knowing the circumstances of the professor's death actually made complete sense for them.

But what about Polly's shock when I told her about the professor's blood-red eyes? Given that she was a plant expert and the poison a type of plant alkaloid, was it possible she had an idea what the poison might be? I made a mental note to tell Matt so he could follow up.

And wasn't *I promise you* an odd thing for Harriet to say? How could she make a commitment like that — unless she was the killer or knew who the killer was? Perhaps she suspected Polly killed the professor and was hoping she'd get away with it and was urging her friend to keep her head down and stay the course to avoid attracting undue attention?

I sighed. What I really needed to do was stop with the speculative nonsense. Every single person I met wasn't the murderer. Words that seemed weighted with hidden meaning were often just empty platitudes. In all likelihood, Harriet simply wanted her friend to stop worrying about a scenario that, in all seriousness, seemed ridiculous and fanciful. And Polly had acted surprised and afraid because murder was frightening. Easy-peasy, nothing to see here, time to move on.

I spent most of the afternoon on the Common helping Mom with an assortment of flower-show tasks — staffing the ticket booth during a volunteer's lunch break, cleaning up a floral display that someone had knocked over, and refilling the coffee urn in the media tent for the journalists now arriving en masse.

As the afternoon sun dipped toward the horizon, Janie texted to tell me she was heading to the cafe to meet the health inspector. After checking with Mom, I left the flower show and joined them. The inspector poked around the kitchen — "nice setup" was his only substantive comment — and cleared us to reopen.

After seeing him out, Janie and I breathed a sigh of relief.

"Back to normal tomorrow?" I said.

She nodded. "It should be a busy day with all the visitors in town."

My phone buzzed — a text from Mayor Johnson. "Congratulations on reopening. Can we order croissants and muffins for the media tent tomorrow morning?"

I showed Janie and she smiled. "Told you."

And just like that, Emily's Eats was back in business.

The day would have ended on that encouraging note were it not for what happened next.

After Janie headed home and I locked up the cafe, I trudged up the stairs to my apartment. Once inside, I set my keys on the credenza in the foyer and flipped on the living room lights. The day had been a busy one and truth be told, I was tired and looking forward to a quiet evening. I was in the kitchen, trying to decide what to do for dinner, when I realized something wasn't right.

But what? I frowned, unsure. Then I saw it: The door to the dumbwaiter shaft was shut tight.

Why was the door closed? Without fail, I kept it open to let Mr. Snuggles come and go as he pleased.

I walked over and yanked it up. As expected, moving the door took effort — it tended to get stuck.

Had it somehow closed on its own? Had Mr. Snuggles figured out a way to pull it down tight?

Unconvinced, I ran my gaze over the rest of the kitchen and then the living room. Was anything else different?

I was looking at Aunt Emily's wall of travel photos and about to move on when I froze.

Was something off?

I stepped closer and breathed in sharply. Among the framed photos on the wall were two from North Africa, one from Morocco showing Emily in a market in Marrakesh, the other from

Egypt showing Emily on a camel, the Great Pyramids in the background.

The Moroccan photo was supposed to be hanging above the Egyptian photo. But now the positions were reversed.

A chill went through me.

Someone had been here.

In the apartment!

With a trembling hand, I pulled out my phone and called Matt.

"Hey," he said, picking up right away. "What's up?"

"I'm at the apartment," I whispered. "Someone broke in."

"Are you okay?" he demanded, instantly on high alert.

"I'm fine."

"Is anyone else there?"

"I don't think so."

"Stay put. I'll be there in two."

As I slid my phone back into my pocket, I realized something. I'd told him I was alone — but was that true? I listened carefully, my heart thumping uncomfortably.

After a full minute of silence, I was ready to conclude that indeed I was alone, but I remained still for another minute until, to my intense relief, I heard footsteps pounding up the hallway stairs. I hurried to the door and flung it open just as Matt reached the landing.

"Are you okay?" he asked breathlessly, pulling me into his arms.

"I'm fine."

"You sure you're alone?"

"Yes. I mean, I think so."

He let me go and searched each room methodically and efficiently, me following in his wake, grateful beyond words that he was here.

After satisfying himself that the apartment was clear, he turned to me. "Show me what's off."

I swallowed back a rush of emotion. He was taking me at my word. He wasn't questioning my judgment. He wasn't assuming I was overreacting or imagining dangers that didn't exist.

"Two things," I said, then showed him the dumbwaiter door and the photos on the travel wall.

"Anything else disturbed or out of place?"

"Not that I noticed."

"Let's go through the apartment again and look for anything that's not right."

I set about my task, walking slowly through each room.

"I'm not seeing anything," I finally said.

He regarded me thoughtfully. "You weren't robbed. Nothing is broken. If the intruders had been a bit more careful, you wouldn't have known they were here."

I swallowed back a rush of fear. "That's right."

"They were looking for something."

"But what?"

He shrugged. "No idea. Something small enough to be hidden inside a picture frame."

That's when I remembered. "Last fall, Emily hid a flash drive for me inside a hollowed-out slot in a picture frame."

Matt walked back to the wall of travel photos and took the Morocco picture off the wall. "This frame's a bit heavier than the others."

I grabbed the Egypt picture and examined the frame closely. "I'm not seeing anything."

After a careful look at his, Matt shook his head. "Me either."

We hung the photos up again and stood there for a moment.

"This feels like a spy thing," he said.

"Yep. If it walks like a duck and quacks like a duck…."

"We need to check the rest of the building."

He was right, I realized. "The entire building was empty today. The cafe was shut down. I was at the flower show most of the afternoon, as was Mr. Benson. Gabby was at the hospital with her gang."

We headed downstairs and searched the basement and the cafe, finding nothing, then went upstairs to the studio apartment. I was about to unlock the door when he said, "Hang on."

He pulled out his phone and made a call. "Quick question," he said after a second. "When you examined the studio apartment in Sarah's building yesterday, did you do your usual?" He listened for a few seconds. "Got it. Thanks."

He hung up and turned to me. "No sharing, but the techs have a trick to help us know when someone ignores orders about staying out of a crime scene."

Oh, dear. The way he'd phrased that, it almost sounded like he thought I might be one of those people who might on occasion be tempted to ignore orders about staying out of crime scenes. He was, of course, completely correct to suspect that, though I couldn't for the life of me recall whether I'd actually ever done it.

I watched him carefully examine a spot on the door about a foot below the handle. "When the techs leave a scene, they glue a hair to the door and door frame."

"So if the hair is gone…."

"Then we know someone went in." He straightened up and turned toward me. "No hair."

"Someone was here."

He stood aside to let me unlock the door.

"I don't know if I'm going to be able to tell you much about what might be moved or missing," I said as we stepped inside.

He surveyed the room. "The techs told me they left everything as they found it."

"Did they discover anything helpful?"

"Aside from noting that the professor was stuck in the past, they said his belongings were unremarkable."

"Stuck in the past," I repeated, my gaze lingering on his steamer trunk and thinking about his old-fashioned clothes. "That's a good way to describe him."

"Old school all the way. I'll have someone clear this out tomorrow."

"No rush."

"I'll feel better when we have his belongings in the evidence shed."

"Let me know when and I'll be here."

He gave me a smile and pulled me into his arms. "About your neighbors," he said.

"Yes?"

"I'd prefer we not bother them with this. It's probably safe to assume their apartments were searched as well, but I doubt we'll find any evidence."

"Makes sense. Plus, if you tell them, they'll blab."

His arms around me tightened. "I don't like you staying here alone."

"I'll be fine," I assured him. "How about this:

I'll invite Mr. Benson and Gabby up for dinner and TV."

He didn't reply right away, his expression serious. "You sure?" he finally said.

"Positive. You're welcome to join, of course."

"I'd love to, but…."

"Another long night?"

"Very long." He leaned in and kissed my forehead. "I want you to call me if anything — and I mean anything — comes up."

"Will do."

CHAPTER 18

That night, I did exactly what I told Matt I'd do — I invited Mr. Benson and Gabby up for dinner and TV and probably kept them up far too late, given the busy day we'd all had.

Fortunately, I slept soundly that night, undisturbed by anything unusual or alarming, and awoke at dawn ready to leap into my normal routine.

Our Saturday morning began at a brisk clip, with our regular cafe crowd joined by a horde of media folks — all of them eager for caffeine, muffins, and interviews with yours truly.

"We read in the *Gazette* that you found the dead body," the reporters all murmured from across the cash register, their voices oozing well-practiced sympathy. "How terrible. What was that like for you?"

The reporters also all said, "We researched the recent homicides in Eagle Cove and your role in capturing the killers. How scary that must have been. What led to your involvement?"

A few also added, "Your cafe appears to be at the epicenter of the recent violence in Eagle Cove. How distressing that must be. What are your thoughts about that?"

To all of them, I replied, "I'm happy to answer any questions you have about the wonderful muffins, croissants, pies and other treats available here at Emily's Eats, but I have no comment about anything else."

Which didn't stop them from pushing. Fortunately, I managed to maintain a patient and courteous facade throughout, even as they probed for cracks in my armor.

By early afternoon, with the cafe finally free of journalists and the morning rush behind us, things were starting to feel more normal. Hialeah was at her table near the window awaiting her next client. Mr. Benson was back from a morning visit to the flower show and on his usual stool at the counter. Gabby was gabbing with Mrs. Chan, Mrs. Bunch, and Ms. Hollingsworth in their favorite red booth, the ladies looking rested and healthy after their night of recovery in the hospital.

The cafe door opened and Claire stepped

inside. After chatting briefly with Gabby and Mr. Benson, she approached me at the register.

"I've kinda been expecting you," I said.

Her expression was serious. "Can we take a quick walk?"

"Now?"

"The weather's nice and I'd like to get some sun."

I poked my head into the kitchen, where Janie was boxing up a fresh batch of muffins. "Hey, okay if I dash out for a few minutes?"

"Sure," she said. "How long?"

"Ten minutes, tops."

"No prob."

"Thanks."

Without another word, I followed Claire out of the building.

She turned left on Main Street, her long strides forcing me to hustle to keep up. "Anything damaged or taken last night?"

"Nope," I said, not bothering to ask how she knew about the break-ins.

"What made you realize you'd had visitors?"

"The dumbwaiter door was shut tight — it's always open — and two of Emily's travel photos were in the wrong places on the wall."

She frowned. "Gabby's? Mr. Benson's?"

"We assume their apartments were searched as well, but we didn't tell them what happened and don't know for sure. The studio apartment was searched."

"And you know that because…?"

"The crime techs placed a hair over the edge of the door when they left."

"A hair that's no longer there."

"Right."

"Basement? Cafe?"

I shrugged. "We looked but didn't notice anything."

Though she was trying to hide it, I could tell she was alarmed.

"You're worried," I said.

She stopped walking and turned to face me directly. "Big-time."

"Why?"

"Something's afoot and we don't know what."

"You gotta give me something. Anything."

She compressed her lips, which is what she did when wrestling with a difficult decision.

"All right," she finally said. "High-level, non-specific, and only because you are you and I am me and I don't know what else to do."

"Got it."

"Decades ago, something happened."

"Wow. So informative."

She ignored me — she'd heard this complaint from me a thousand times. "Recent events have shown the risks weren't fully contained and the something is still very much a clear and present danger."

"Is the something why Emily was pulled out of retirement?"

She hesitated. "We shouldn't be talking about this."

"Yet here we are."

She regarded me for a moment, clearly torn. "Emily was reactivated when it became clear the threat still exists."

"Which is why Professor Greeley was also reactivated and sent here?"

"And why I've been up here a lot as well."

"How do the metal boxes from the lake tie in?"

She sighed. "I can't tell you that."

"But they do tie in, right?"

"Sarah…."

"The scientists who were killed a few months ago — they were part of it?"

She shook her head. "Not part of it, no. The events in question occurred decades ago."

"But they found out something related?"

Another nod.

"And tried to profit from their knowledge?"

Another nod.

"A lot of people inside H.U.S.H. seem to know about these long-ago events. That worries you."

Claire's expression became guarded. "I'm not sure why you say that."

"A small thing. When you arranged for the professor to stay in the studio apartment, you didn't set it up through the travel agency that H.U.S.H. normally uses. Instead, you went to the mayor and the mayor called me."

"Sarah…."

"At first, I thought you set it up that way because you didn't want me to know the professor was associated with H.U.S.H."

She didn't reply.

"But now I see you did it because you didn't want certain people in H.U.S.H. knowing you'd reactivated the professor."

Claire's lips tightened.

"You don't trust your own agency."

"We shouldn't be discussing this," she said quietly.

"There are traitors in H.U.S.H. and you don't know who they are."

She looked around to make sure no one was listening. "When I say you have to stop, I mean it. What's going on is not a game. We're up against a conspiracy that goes back decades. We don't know who's involved. The danger is real. The stakes couldn't be higher."

"You don't know who you can trust."

Her silence spoke volumes.

"I assume you trust Emily."

"Of course."

"And Edgar."

"Of course."

I hesitated for a second, as I always did before asking about Claire's ex-husband, who was also an agent. "What about Ben?"

"Of course. And a few others."

"And of course you know you can trust me."

She grunted with irritation. "You saying that — that's the problem in a nutshell. You act like you're part of the team, but you're not. You are *not* a trained agent."

"I'm here to help. Any way I can."

"You can help by staying out of it."

"Of course," I said right away.

Claire frowned. "I want you to mean it."

I opened my mouth to offer a soothing lie, but no words came out, because what could I say? Claire knew me too well.

My childhood best friend fixed me with a glare that I'll admit was impressively fierce. "In the past seven months, you've almost been murdered twice. You just got poisoned with a rare hallucinogen. People who care about you — your daughter, mother, sister, aunt, boyfriend, and close friends — want you to stop putting yourself in harm's way."

As the words flowed, I wondered: Did she really think the guilt card was gonna work? She'd have to do a lot better than that.

"So that's what you think Matt is?" I said. "My boyfriend?"

"Stop deflecting," she snapped.

"I'm not —"

"You are." She looked like she wanted to continue her safety lecture, but she stopped and took a deep breath. "When it comes to Matt, call him whatever you want. Go at your own pace. Do what feels right."

"Thank you."

"You're welcome."

"So I take it you approve?"

Her gaze softened. "Of course I approve. I always have. You two are made for each other."

We stared at each other for a long moment. That's the thing about old friends. Sometimes, even when at odds, words aren't necessary.

"You know," I finally said. "I'd be more help if I knew what everyone is after."

"Maybe. But I'm not going to tell you."

"Boo."

She looked so tall, so sleek, so gorgeous, so formidable as she stood there glaring at me.

"I'm serious about this, Sarah." A pleading note crept into her voice. "For once, please listen to me. For your sake and mine, stay out of this."

Her phone chose that moment to buzz. She looked at it and grimaced.

"More good news?"

She gave me a tight smile. "Can we continue this later?"

"Of course."

I watched her walk away, then turned and headed back to the cafe.

When I stepped inside, I saw that Matt was there — yay! — along with someone I'd hoped to avoid.

"Good afternoon, Sarah," Wendy said, her gaze slightly predatory. "I'd like to continue our discussion from yesterday."

"I'm not sure I can right now," I said, glancing about for something I could claim as an urgent task. "There's a lot of stuff I need to do."

Wendy was about to call me on my nonsense when we heard Mr. Benson clear his throat. "Sheriff Forsyth, I'm glad you're here. There's something I need to tell you."

I went still. Mr. Benson's tone sounded serious. Wendy's attention shifted to him, her reportorial instincts all a-quiver.

Matt gave Mr. Benson his full attention. "What is it, Donald?"

Mr. Benson took a deep breath to fortify himself, then said:

"I'm the one who did it, Sheriff. I killed Professor Greeley."

CHAPTER 19

To say that Mr. Benson's announcement landed like a bomb would be an understatement. The entire cafe froze. Bewildered looks were exchanged. Surely we'd misheard. Perhaps he was just making a bad joke?

But no.

The bomb-thrower eased off his stool and straightened his bow tie. "What happened was inadvertent, Sheriff. Harm was not my intent. But I'm the one who added the poison to Professor Greeley's teacup."

For a long moment, no one spoke. Was this for real?

Matt's expression was serious. "Donald, do you know what you're saying?"

"Most certainly."

"Hogwash!" Gabby cried, springing into action,

her cane clacking as she scrambled out of the booth. "Shut your trap, you old crank. Not another word."

Mr. Benson shook his head. "I have a duty to tell the sheriff what occurred, Gabby."

"Bah." She pushed her way between the two men and glared at Matt. "He's gaga. Confused. An idiot. A raving lunatic."

"Gabby," Mr. Benson began.

"Don't 'Gabby' me, you old fool," she snapped, her eyes still on Matt. "You let him be, you hear? Man's mad as a hatter."

Matt sighed. "Donald, let's discuss this at the station."

"Thank you, Sheriff," Mr. Benson said.

Before they could move an inch, Gabby zipped to the cafe door and blocked it with her cane. "This is police harassment. Elder abuse!"

Matt sighed again. "Sarah, we'll leave through the other door."

Before Gabby could stop them, he and Mr. Benson exited the cafe via the hallway.

"You have the right to remain silent, you moron!" Gabby yelled as the door shut behind them. "Don't you dare say another word!"

And then, just like that, they were gone, leaving the rest of us flabbergasted and speechless.

The cafe's front door opened and I turned around in time to see Wendy dashing away.

Oh, dear. Mr. Benson had handed her a huge scoop. I could already see tomorrow's *Gazette* headline: *Killer Confesses — Case Solved!*

"Sarah," Gabby said, whirling toward me. "You have to stop him."

I shrugged helplessly. "I'm sorry, but I don't see —"

"Bah." Disgusted, she turned to her crew in the booth. "Girls, we have work to do. Upstairs!"

Mrs. Chen, Mrs. Bunch, and Ms. Hollingsworth hurried out of the booth and, after throwing disappointed looks my way, marched out of the cafe, their angry footsteps vibrating through the building as they stomped upstairs to Gabby's apartment.

Completely flummoxed, I turned to Janie and Hialeah, hoping one of them had a grip on what had just happened.

Hialeah's stricken gaze told me she was as lost as I was. "Sarah, you don't think Donald said that to … help someone?"

"Not a clue," I replied, though her guess was certainly a possibility. My mind starting churning again. "Honestly, in a million years, I never would have…."

"He is such a caring soul."

Janie was shaking her head. "When he said the poisoning was 'inadvertent,' what did he mean?"

"Great question," I said immediately. "I mean,

how can he be sure about anything he did at the reception? He was high as a kite. He barely remembers doing the hula. His memory is as scrambled as mine."

"And what he did — it's not like him."

My heart thumped — Janie was making an excellent point. "You mean, it's not his style to make dramatic announcements like that?"

"He would take Matt aside and discuss the matter with him privately."

I fervently agreed. Something was going on — something I didn't know about. Mr. Benson had an agenda.

A plan began forming. I whipped out my phone and texted Matt. "Something's off. Can I talk with him?"

I turned to Janie and Hialeah. "Listen, if we want to help Mr. Benson, then we need to consider alternatives."

Hialeah's brow furrowed. "You mean, identify other suspects?"

"Well," I said, taking a breath as I gathered my thoughts, "I was thinking more about witnesses. People who know more than they're letting on."

Hialeah went still. "People like who?"

I kept my tone steady. "People like you, Hialeah. It's time for you to tell us how you knew Professor Greeley."

Hialeah's cheeks flushed. "What?"

"I'm sorry," I said, trying to sound gentle but firm, "but we need to know. His arrival in Eagle Cove upset you. We need to know why. You're in a safe place. It's just the three of us — you, me, and Janie."

Her eyes filled with tears. "I'm sorry. I can't. I just can't."

And then, to my utter astonishment —

She rose to her feet and ran out of the cafe!

Janie stared at the cafe door as it swung shut, stunned. "How do you know she knew Professor Greeley?"

"I didn't, at least not for sure."

"You definitely struck a nerve. I hope she's okay."

"Should I go after her?"

Janie was about to answer when my phone buzzed. Matt had texted back: "Agree. Come to the station right now."

I turned to Janie. "Matt wants me to go to the station."

"Good. I hope you can sort this out. I'll hold down the fort."

I grabbed my handbag and dashed out. The sheriff's station was a six-minute walk or a two-minute drive. With no time to waste, I hurried to my SUV and zoomed away.

On the short drive over, I tried to sort out my thoughts. It felt like I'd been hit by a tornado.

Barely thirty minutes ago, the cafe had been full of folks behaving more or less normally.

Then — *bam*. In the space of two minutes:

Mr. Benson dropped his bomb and left with Matt.

Wendy dashed off with her scoop.

Gabby erupted and marched upstairs with her pals.

Hialeah burst into tears and ran away.

And now here I was, racing across town to help a self-confessed accidental killer — a dear, sweet man who was very likely hiding something.

As I swung into the parking lot across the street from the sheriff's station, I found myself getting rather upset. Eagle Cove didn't deserve the mess it was in. Hadn't enough already happened to our poor town? When were the surprises going to end?

By the time I turned off the engine, I'd managed to work myself into a lather. My lower lip was trembling. I felt jangly, on edge.

Calm thyself down, I ordered myself. *One thing at a time. Remember why you're here. You need to find out what Mr. Benson is up to.*

While waiting for my composure to return, I focused on the two-story brick building that housed the sheriff's station and jail. Built in the late 1800s, it was a straightforward structure compared to the ornate Victorians on either side. Its red brick walls, narrow windows, and double-front oak doors gave it a heavy, solid feel. Matt had included a funding request for renovations in his budget for the coming fiscal year and I hoped the money came through, because — keeping it honest here — the place needed spiffing up.

With a sigh, I hopped out of my SUV and hurried across the street into the station.

Deputy Paul was at the reception desk. Behind him, the main room — an open space with a bunch of desks and chairs and normally bustling with people — was empty.

"Afternoon, Deputy," I said. "I take it everyone else is busy elsewhere?"

"Afternoon, Ms. Boone," he replied, his youthful face strained with exhaustion. "Yeah, we're stretched pretty thin."

"I'm here because…."

He gestured to the stairs. "They're waiting for you."

"Thank you."

I hurried upstairs to the second floor, which included Matt's office, the station's interrogation room, and the conference room where I found Matt and Mr. Benson.

They both looked up as I stepped in.

Matt glanced at his phone. "I have to take a call. Okay if I leave you two alone for a few minutes?"

"Of course," I said.

Matt's expression as he stepped past me said it all: *Please get what you can from him.*

After Matt walked to his office two doors down and closed his door, I turned toward Mr. Benson.

"I'm glad you're here," he whispered, gesturing to a chair next to him. "I need to tell you something, but I can't risk anyone overhearing."

After closing the conference room door, I sat down next to him, curious and alarmed. He was shaking with barely suppressed emotion. A storm was raging inside him and only through sustained effort was he managing to keep it from escaping and wreaking havoc.

"What I'm about to tell you must be kept a secret. You must promise me."

"Mr. Benson —"

"You deserve to know. But first I must have your word."

My stomach was in knots. What in the world was going on? What could he possibly want to tell me?

"I promise," I said.

He took a deep breath and whispered:

"Your Aunt Emily is *alive.*"

CHAPTER 20

I couldn't help myself — I gasped. Panic raced through me. The last thing I'd expected Mr. Benson to say was *that*.

How in the world did he know?

My shock must have been apparent because he reached out and gave my hand a sympathetic squeeze. "Sarah, I know this comes as a tremendous surprise."

"You have no idea," I managed to say.

"I didn't know what to make of it either, at least not at first."

I tried to wrap my head around his words. "Why do you believe Emily is alive?"

"She told me herself."

I breathed in sharply. Emily had reached out to Mr. Benson without giving me a heads-up? "You spoke with her?"

"Not exactly."

"Then how did she tell you?"

He pulled back, as if suddenly regretting his decision to share his Emily news with me.

"Please, Mr. Benson. You opened the door. I promise I won't tell anyone."

Slowly, he reached into one of his socks and pulled out a folded piece of paper.

"She sent me a letter," he whispered.

Another jolt went through me — this time of recognition. Emily was fond of using letters to communicate. The previous autumn, she'd sent me two letters from beyond her so-called grave.

After glancing around to make sure we were still alone, Mr. Benson handed me the letter.

As I opened it, I couldn't restrain another gasp — the handwriting looked like Emily's.

Hands trembling, I read:

Donald,

This letter will shock you and for that I am truly sorry. The last thing I wish is to cause you distress.

I am alive and must ask for your help.

You are wondering how this letter can be real. As you assess its validity, remember this: You know my handwriting. You know me. You know my past. You know that what I've written in this letter is more than possible.

What I can share is this: With the assistance of my

previous employer, I faked my death and once again am quietly engaged in matters of international importance.

The help I need from you comes in two parts.

The first part must happen immediately. Go to the sheriff right away — time is of the essence — and tell him you inadvertently poisoned Professor Greeley. Tell him the following: Shortly after the reception began, you and the professor were discussing orchids when the professor handed you his teacup and asked you to find some sugar for it. You spotted a sugar jar at a nearby table, added a spoonful to the professor's cup, and handed the cup back to the professor. You watched the professor take a sip from his cup. When you parted ways a short time later, the professor was still very much alive.

The sheriff will question you closely. He will press for details. I urge you to stick to this story and avoid embellishing. Tell him the encounter was brief. Tell him you don't recall the exact time of the conversation. Tell him you approached the professor with a question about your orchid entry in the competition. Tell him the professor responded rudely. Tell him you don't remember what the sugar jar looked like. When the sheriff asks how you knew the sugar jar contained the poison, tell him you put two and two together.

The second part of this request must take place Monday evening, the day after the flower show ends. Hand this letter to the sheriff and explain everything in full. Hold nothing back.

Before Monday evening, you must not share this letter

or its contents with anyone. The timing and need for secrecy are vitally important.

I know you have questions. Due to circumstances I am not at liberty to explain, I am unable to provide answers at this time.

What I can share is why your help is needed. I worked with Polly Pence and can attest to her good character. Decades ago, she and Beauregard Greeley dated briefly. When she discovered he was married, she ended the relationship. In retaliation, he went out of his way to punish her. For several painful years, she was subjected to an anonymous harassment campaign — a campaign she is sure was Greeley's doing.

She's made every effort to avoid him since — no easy matter in the insular horticultural world. Had she known he would be in Eagle Cove, she never would have agreed to judge our flower show. The night before his death, he got her alone and threatened her again. Panicked, she made a decision she now regrets. Using her horticultural expertise, she extracted a potent hallucinogen from an orchid in the competition. Her plan was to disorient Greeley long enough to escape. She had no intention of killing him or dosing anyone else and is terribly sorry about that. She needs time to return home and arrange her affairs. In particular, she needs to ensure proper care for her elderly mother before surrendering herself to the authorities.

Please do not ask Polly about her involvement in Greeley's death, and please do not tell her about me or *this letter. Polly retired from her former job many years ago. She does not know I am alive.*

Your friendship means the world to me, Donald. I hope you will agree to help Polly in her time of need.

When I see you next, I promise I will explain everything.

With much love and appreciation,
Emily

A jumble of emotions coursed through me as I absorbed what I was reading. So much of the letter rang true. Yet how could it be?

Mr. Benson was watching me anxiously. "It's her handwriting, Sarah," he whispered. "I'm sure of it."

"It does look like hers."

"It also sounds like her."

Indeed, the letter was vintage Emily: clear, firm, persuasive, thoughtful, caring, determined.

I needed time to think this through. And I needed more information. "How and when did you get it?"

"At the flower show this morning, a man bumped into me. After apologizing, he handed me the letter and said, 'I think you dropped this.' Before I could correct him, he vanished into the crowd."

"What did he look like?"

"White, brown hair, thirties, dressed casually."

"Ordinary, in other words?"

"Like a suburban dad."

"Would you recognize him if you saw him again?"

"I believe so."

"Okay, go on."

"From the instant I opened the letter, from the handwriting alone" — his voice picked up with excitement — "I knew."

"And —"

"I decided right away to provide Polly with the help Emily requested."

"Mr. Benson, I'm not sure that's —"

"Sarah," he said, cutting me off. "Polly is the primary caregiver for her mother. She needs time to organize alternate arrangements."

"Yes, but —"

"Polly mentioned her mother in conversation yesterday. What the letter says about Polly's mother is correct."

"But confessing to something you didn't do…."

He straightened his back. "I'm helping a friend."

"But you could end up in jail."

"Only for a night or two. A minor inconvenience."

"But you aren't guilty of anything."

"Sarah," he said, vibrating with excitement. "You seem to have missed the most incredible part of this: Emily is *alive*. Isn't that wonderful?"

Indeed, it was wonderful. He looked so elated. Did I dare acknowledge the truth about Emily without first confirming that the letter was real?

"It's amazing if it's true," I told him. "But don't you think we need to learn more before we accept the letter at face value?"

"The handwriting is hers. The words are hers."

I swallowed, sympathizing with the firmness of his convictions yet unable to ignore the feeling I was missing something. "Can I borrow the letter?"

"No, Sarah. I'm going to do what Emily asked me to do. I will keep this letter secret until I give it to the sheriff on Monday evening."

"Can I at least take a photo of it?" Before he could say no, I added, "I want to study it and I want to help. Please?"

"You've already promised you won't share this information with anyone."

"Yes, I promised that."

"Do you promise to keep that promise?"

"Of course." The lie came easily — too easily.

"Very well." He opened the letter and waited for me to aim my phone at it.

I was still getting the focus right when I heard footsteps in the hall. Hurriedly, I snapped a photo as Mr. Benson slipped the letter back into his sock.

"Do you think they'll search me and find the letter?" he whispered.

I gave myself a mental kick for not thinking of

that thirty seconds earlier and persuading him to give me the letter for safekeeping.

"I doubt it," I whispered as Matt returned to the room.

At the sight of us, Matt went still. No doubt we looked like the guilty co-conspirators we were as we stared at him anxiously, fake smiles plastered on our faces.

"Donald," he said, pretending not to notice. "That was the prosecutor. We won't be pressing charges quite yet, but I'd like you to remain at the station while we investigate further."

I sat upright and pretended to be outraged. "Matt, surely that's not necessary."

"Sorry, Sarah. Given the unknowns, it's best Donald stay here for now."

Mr. Benson rose to his feet. "I understand, Sheriff. If you don't mind, I'd like to lie down. It's been a tiring day."

"I'll take you to a cell." As he led Mr. Benson out, Matt shot me a look whose meaning was perfectly clear: *Don't leave. We need to talk.*

I would have loved to do just that. Yet I knew I couldn't.

The instant Matt and Mr. Benson were out of sight, I grabbed my handbag and raced out of the station.

CHAPTER 21

I dashed to my car and drove away as fast as I could. The instant the station was in my rear-view mirror, I called Mom.

"We need to have a talk with you-know-who," I told her the second she picked up.

"Not now, dear. There are a million things going on and I —"

"I'm sorry, but we have to. Mr. Benson said he killed Professor Greeley."

"Yes, dear, I heard. It's awful."

"He also said you-know-who told him to say that."

"Wait." It took her a second. "He said *what?*"

"Exactly. I'm heading to your house. Get there as soon as you can."

My next call was to Claire and went pretty much the exact same way, almost word for word.

The reason the three of us needed to meet at Mom's house was that the only way Mom and I could talk with Emily was via Mom's computer in Mom's kitchen. This was due to security protections installed by H.U.S.H. on her computer (or in her house, I wasn't sure) to allow for encrypted communications with Emily wherever she happened to be.

After the usual slow-mo traffic through downtown, I hit the main county road and sped up. A few minutes later, I turned onto Maple Drive. The homes here, built on small lots after World War II, were modest and lovingly maintained. The winding streets and mature trees gave the neighborhood a settled-in quality, like it knew what it was about and was content with that.

After parking in front of Mom's snug two-story house, I hustled inside and headed straight for the kitchen — more specifically, to the kitchen table in the nook overlooking the back patio.

The kitchen table was where Mom kept her laptop. I opened it and went to the website that served as the starting point for the secret communications system that H.U.S.H. had set up for Mom and Emily.

After typing in the password, I waited.

A chat window popped up. "What do you want?"

Not exactly a friendly greeting, but I went ahead

and typed, "Mom, Claire, and I need to talk with Emily."

The H.U.S.H. operator typed, "Is this an emergency?"

"Not life-and-death. But yes, it's important."

"Where are Claire and Nancy?"

"On their way."

"We'll connect you when they arrive."

And just like that, the chat window vanished.

I let out a sigh. As always, it was disconcerting to be reminded that H.U.S.H. would know when Claire and Mom arrived. I glanced around the kitchen, wondering for the millionth time where H.U.S.H. had hidden the secret cameras and microphones that simply had to be here somewhere.

My phone buzzed. I looked at it.

Matt.

Oh boy. I'd hoped to avoid talking with him right now — he was way too good at sussing out my evasions. A single hesitation and he'd know I was hiding something.

On the flip side, if I didn't pick up, he'd *definitely* know.

Steeling myself, I accepted the call. "Hey, Matt. What's up?"

"I was expecting you to stick around for a bit."

"I thought I could, but Mom called," I said, the lie coming easily and sounding pretty good to my ears. "She left something at the house and asked me to run out to get it."

"You there now? I can meet you."

"No need," I said immediately. "I'll come to you. How about I swing by the station?"

After a short pause, he said, "Sorry, something's come up. Gotta go. See you soon?"

"Sounds great."

Then he was gone.

I rewound the call in my head. Had I said anything that might set off an alarm? Had I successfully communicated my complete and utter lack of sneaky subterfuge?

You're probably good, I reassured myself. I glanced around for something to keep me busy. Mom kept a clean kitchen, but in the sink I noticed a plate and coffee mug. Pleased to have a distraction, I rinsed them off and set them in the dishwasher. The dishwasher had enough plates and glasses in it to justify a wash, so I added soap, closed the lid tight, and hit the start button.

As the dishwasher roared to life — it's an older model and on the noisy side — I caught the faint sound of the front door closing.

"Sarah," Mom said as she bustled into the kitchen. "Why in the world would Emily ask Donald to confess to murder?"

Her stare was anxious, her bewilderment clear.

"I don't know. We need to ask Emily."

"Why would she tell him she's still alive? She told us not to tell a soul."

"I'm as surprised as you are."

"So the plan is to ask Emily?"

"As soon as Claire arrives."

Mom put her handbag on the kitchen table and sat down heavily in front of the laptop. She looked tired. The swirl of events was catching up with her.

She took a deep breath, then exhaled. Then did it again.

"What's with the deep breathing?" I said after watching her repeat herself four times.

She opened her eyes. "Stress reduction technique."

"I didn't know you were into that."

"There are a lot of things you don't know about your mother, dear."

I blinked with surprise, her words generating a rush of unexpected emotion. What she'd said was true. I'd left Eagle Cove a quarter-century ago and been back barely half a year. In ways large and small, Mom and I were still playing catch-up on all we'd missed in each other's lives.

"How about I make us some tea?" I said.

"Thank you. That sounds lovely."

I was setting the kettle on the stove when I caught movement on the back patio through the kitchen windows. Claire had arrived.

"Oh, good," Mom said as she went to the kitchen door and let her in.

Claire stepped inside and shut the door behind her. "Got here as soon as I could. I knocked at the front door but" — she gestured to the dishwasher — "I guessed you couldn't hear?"

"That thing is so loud," Mom said apologetically. "I keep saying I need a new one, but there's never enough time to figure out which one to get."

"Speaking of time," I said, reaching for mugs. "I know we're all busy, so let's get to it. Claire, you want tea?"

"No thanks — I'm good."

Mom sat down at the table and stared at the laptop. "We're all here now," she said out loud.

I blinked, startled. "You don't have to type in your password?"

She shrugged. "They know me."

A man's voice, sounding friendly, came from the computer. "Good afternoon, Nancy."

Mom smiled. "How are you, Kenneth?"

"Fine, ma'am. Had that talk with my dad and it went pretty well. Just like you hoped it would."

"Oh, good. I'm so glad."

Claire and I exchanged glances, which Mom noticed.

"Kenneth's a very nice young man," she explained.

"You and Kenneth talk?" I asked.

"While we're waiting for Emily. Like now."

"What was that about his dad?"

She threw me an exasperated look. "That's really none of your business, Sarah."

From the computer, Kenneth said, "She's joining now, ma'am. Have a good day. And thanks again."

"Talk with you soon."

A video window popped up as Claire and I stepped behind Mom.

And then, from wherever in the world she happened to be in that moment, Aunt Emily was with us. Her thin, angular face filled the screen, her intelligent grey eyes alive with concern. "Nancy, Sarah, Claire, I'm told there's a need for urgent discussion?"

She looked and sounded good, her voice clear and strong. In previous calls, she'd had a bandage on the left side of her forehead over the scar she'd received during her near-fatal car crash seven months earlier. But now the bandage was gone and the scar barely visible. She'd put on makeup and was dressed in a black dress and pearls, as if heading for an evening out.

The room behind her was elegant, with French doors opening onto what looked like a large balcony. The sky outside was dark, which told me she was several time zones ahead — Europe, most likely. I imagined her someplace exciting and glamorous like Barcelona, Rome, Paris, or London.

Mom cleared her throat. "Things are crazy here, Emily."

"I heard about Greeley," Emily replied, her tone crisp. "But that's not why you're calling."

I jumped in. "Emily, I'll start. Did you send a letter to Mr. Benson?"

Emily shook her head. "I did not."

"Well, someone did." I recounted my conversation with Mr. Benson in full while Emily, Mom, and Claire listened attentively.

"I can't believe this is happening," Mom said when I finished.

On the stove, the kettle whistled. I dashed over and poured steaming water into two mugs.

Claire was pacing back and forth in the not-very-big kitchen, deep in problem-solving mode. "Someone handed him the letter at the flower show this morning?"

"That's what he said."

"I'll ask if" — she almost said Edgar's name, but stopped herself in time, since Mom didn't know about Edgar — "we captured any video footage that might be relevant."

"The letter says Polly Pence used to work at H.U.S.H. Is that true?"

Claire shot a glance at Emily, who said, "Many years ago, yes. She was a researcher, not an agent."

"Did you know her?"

"No. We overlapped only briefly — she started shortly before I left."

"Is it possible she's the killer? Or the letter-writer? Or both?"

"It's possible, yes," Claire said. "We'll look into it."

"Sarah," Emily said from the video screen. "You said the handwriting looked like mine."

"Yes," I said, still at the counter with the two mugs of tea. "But more than that. The words, the tone — the letter *sounded* like you."

"Then it must have been written by someone who knows me and my handwriting."

"Also," Mom added, "the letter-writer knows things about the reception. He or she was there."

Claire stopped pacing and turned to Emily. "If that's right, then…."

"Agreed," Emily said quietly.

"Which means…."

"I'll let them know right away."

I frowned. Claire and Emily did this sometimes — got oblique and vague and let their sentences trail off. I knew why, of course — they didn't want me and Mom knowing about their Big Bad Secret. I couldn't help but feel irritated.

After all, I was in this thing up to my eyeballs. In seven short months I'd discovered four dead bodies, helped catch two killers, and nearly been murdered twice. More importantly, I'd kept their secrets. Hadn't I proved I could be trusted? Hadn't I demonstrated how helpful I could be? When were they going to stop withholding information and allow me into their inner circle?

Emily's focus swung to me. "Sarah, do you have the letter?"

"Mr. Benson wouldn't give it to me. But I snapped a photo." I took out my phone and showed it to Claire and Mom.

"Sarah, it's blurry," Mom said.

"Sorry, I was rushed. Matt was about to walk back in."

"I can barely make out the words."

"Sarah," Emily said, "email the photo to Claire. We'll get the techs on it."

At the edge of my awareness, I detected a faint sound. A knock? "Hey, did anyone hear something? Maybe the front door?"

"Maybe a package delivery," Mom said. "Can you check?"

I hustled down the hallway and opened the front door. No one was there. I was about to shut it when I froze.

Matt's truck was parked in front of the house.

I gasped. Matt was *here?*

In a flash, I knew where he'd gone. As a regular visitor, he knew that when the dishwasher was going, we didn't always hear knocks at the front door.

Desperately, I dashed outside and raced around the house. "Matt, wait!"

With mounting panic, I reached the backyard

—

And found him on the patio.

Staring into the kitchen through the windows.

At Mom and Claire, who were oblivious and chatting away —

With Emily.

Who was clearly visible on the computer screen.

Emily saw him first and said something. Claire and Mom whirled around.

For a long moment, the five of us stood there, frozen.

The five of us had known each other for decades — supported each other, loved each other, trusted each other.

And now one of us had discovered he'd been lied to.

Big-time.

By the rest of us.

By *me*.

"Matt," I said weakly, my heart hammering away.

He tore his gaze from the scene inside and whirled on me with an anger and hurt I'd hoped I'd never see.

"So that's how it is?" he said, his voice raw.

"Matt, I —"

Without another word, he rushed past me. I stood there unable to move, frozen in place, as seconds seemed to extend into eternity.

Frantically, Claire and Mom gestured for me to chase after him. By the time I ran to the front of the house, it was too late.

My heart in my throat, I watched helplessly as his truck roared away.

CHAPTER 22

The kitchen convo broke up right after that. All of us had places to be and tasks to complete.

Before dispersing, we quickly discussed the brand-new problem of Matt.

"He looked so upset," Mom said, her worried gaze on me.

"He'll be fine," Claire said. "He thinks before he acts."

"He's a reasonable and generous man," Emily said. "He'll come around in the end."

Then they all turned to me, their directive clear: *Make sure we're right.*

Which meant I had a new top priority: finessing the reaction of the man I'd lied to.

I drove away from the house feeling terrible, the knot in my stomach growing by the second. I'd messed up. My lie wasn't small — it was *big* and had been going on for *months*. The disbelief and hurt on his face had been painful to see. He'd placed his full trust in me — yet I hadn't reciprocated.

His truck wasn't at the sheriff's station. I cruised the streets of downtown looking for him — no luck. I called and texted, then called and texted again — no reply.

I couldn't really blame him for avoiding me. Had our positions been switched, I probably would have done the same. He needed time to sort things out. As Claire had noted, he thought things through before acting.

Finally, after driving up and down the streets of downtown too many times, I gave up and returned to the cafe. I told Janie that Mr. Benson was staying at the station for now to help Matt with the investigation. We then reviewed the next day's task list before she headed home. I didn't tell her about Mr. Benson's letter or Matt, because how could I? She knew even less about the spy stuff than Matt did. Guilt stabbed through me as I thought about everything I hadn't shared with her.

The late afternoon sun was fading fast. The final customers of the day came and went. I was wiping down tables and getting ready to close when Gabby shuffled in through the hallway door, ignoring me as she moved briskly to her favored booth.

"Don't mind me," she said gruffly. "I'm not even here."

She settled in and sat there like a stone, quiet and still. I frowned, unsure what to make of her behavior. Gabby wasn't one for silent reflection. It was almost like —

Aha.

It was almost like she knew something was coming and wanted a front-row seat.

"Can I get you anything?"

She waved me away. "All good."

I heard the familiar ring of the cafe's front doorbell and turned to see Mom stepping inside. She glanced around the cafe and frowned when she saw Gabby.

"Betsy," Mom muttered under her breath.

"I'm here for moral support," Gabby said.

Mom closed the door and sighed, as if accepting the inevitable.

I regarded the two of them with a mixture of irritation and resignation. The Eagle Cove communications network — one of the most fearsomely effective on the planet — had been blazing away at light speed. Mom had said something to her friend Betsy, Betsy had said something to Gabby, and now Mom and Gabby were both here.

It didn't take a genius to figure out what — in other words, *who* — they'd been talking about.

Mom gestured to the cafe door. "Sarah, is it okay if I...?"

"Sure," I said reluctantly, even as my irritation increased. Was now really the right time for whatever Mom was planning?

She flipped the "Open" sign to "Closed," locked the door, and pointed to the booth. "Do you have a moment?"

I hesitated. I was about to get an old-fashioned talking-to. In front of a witness. Did I want that?

"Mom, as you know, there's stuff I —"

"I know, dear. This won't take long."

From her spot in the booth, Gabby watched, still as a statue.

Mom slid in next to her.

With a sigh, I scooted in opposite.

Almost like a conjurer, Gabby seemed to fade into the background.

Mom fixed me with an expression I knew all too well — her "I'm about to deliver some hard truths" stare.

Briefly, I wondered how she was going to say whatever she was planning to say. With Gabby hanging on her every word, she couldn't bring up anything related to Emily or espionage.

She sat up straight and cleared her throat. "You know I think the world of you, dear."

Uh oh — starting out with a compliment was never a good sign.

"Glad to hear," I murmured carefully.

"You're so smart, so organized, so generous, always looking out for others...."

Oh, boy — this was gonna be bad. "Thank you?"

"But sometimes...." Her gaze grew more intense. "Sometimes you miss things — things that others see more clearly."

"Things such as...?"

"Well," she said, taking a deep breath. "Like with Matt."

Here it was — the opening salvo. "What about Matt?"

"You're holding back with him."

"If you mean what we were talking about earlier, I know," I said, mindful of Gabby's presence and hoping to bring this moment of maternal inspection to a swift conclusion. "I don't see that I had a choice."

"No, dear. That's not what I meant."

"Then what did you mean?"

"You've been holding back with him *emotionally*."

Okay, that surprised me. Mom hadn't stuck her nose into my Matt business much, which I appreciated. Yet here she was doing just that and taking his side to boot.

"Mom, I —"

"Please, dear, let me finish. I want to make sure this comes out the right way."

"Okay," I said, adopting a pose of infinite patience. "Go on."

She took another breath. "You developed some bad habits in the final years of your marriage."

I blinked, again surprised.

"When things went south, you pulled back, retreated into your shell, withheld. You didn't share when you should have. You didn't ask for help when you needed to."

The words stung. I felt myself flush.

"I understand why you did that," Mom continued. "You didn't want us worrying about you."

"That's right."

"You did it to protect us. To keep us from being distressed."

"That's right."

"But what you didn't understand was that we *wanted* to help. It was important to us. We *wanted* to be there for you."

She looked so earnest as she said it, her lovely hazel eyes alive with concern and compassion. I felt a rush of warmth as I considered how my divorce must have looked from the outside.

"Mom, I'm sorry about that — truly. You're right. I didn't want to put my stuff on you."

"I know, dear. And I appreciate why. But there was more going on than just that, wasn't there?"

"More? Like what?"

"The divorce — it embarrassed you. It made you feel ashamed."

I flushed. The inspection was turning into a full-on excavation. "Mom, I —"

"You believed what happened was at least partly your fault — that if you had seen the warning signs sooner, if you'd handled things differently, if you'd been more open or forgiving, you could have saved your marriage."

I didn't answer, because what could I say? Every single word hit home. My chest tightened.

Her gaze was gentle but unyielding. "I can only imagine how difficult it was for you to go through all that. What I hope is that you can stop blaming yourself."

"Mom —"

"Bottom line, your former husband betrayed the trust you placed in him. That's on him, one thousand percent."

"I agree, but —"

"Yes, I know — marriage is a two-way street, it takes two to tango, yada yada. But not in this case. Not when your husband cut you out and left you behind. Not when he stole from your daughter. Not when he doubled down when you dared to question him. Not when he refused to ask for your forgiveness."

I couldn't help but appreciate the

comprehensiveness of her summary of Ethan's many failures.

"Thank you, Mom. I'm glad I have your support. Going forward, I promise to do better when it comes to sharing what's troubling me."

"Good," she replied. "Now about Matt."

I restrained a sigh. The digging wasn't done. "What about him?"

"Do you think he's a delicate flower?"

I blinked — another curveball. "Of course not."

"Do you believe he isn't strong enough to deal with your emotions?"

I began to see where she was headed. "That's not what I —"

"Do you think he's unaware of what you're going through?"

"No, of course not. it's just that —"

"Because he's pretty good at reading people."

"Of course he is, but —"

"But what?" She reached across the table and took hold of my hands. "But what, Sarah?"

It took me a long time to reply. The warmth of her grip was reassuring, but also a reminder that she expected the truth. And while I knew the answer to her question — believe me, after her excavation, I knew — getting the words to leave my mouth took effort.

Finally, I spoke. "I don't want to dump my pain on him."

"That's right. That's the pattern you need to break."

"He deserves better from me."

"No, dear." Her voice was soft. "He deserves *more* from you."

Without warning, tears threatened. I tried to blink them away. "Mom, I —"

"Hush, dear. He deserves every part of you, not just the bright, shiny, happy parts."

The advice was spot-on. And also unexpected, coming from her. When it came to Matt and me, she'd always been conspicuously hands-off.

I was about to ask her what had changed when she said, "I haven't pushed you with Matt. As much as I adore him, I haven't been completely comfortable with the idea of you dating him. Law enforcement is a dangerous profession. Anyone in a relationship with him will always be worrying about him."

"Mom…."

"I also needed to see how you two were with each other — whether you were still right for each other, even after all these years."

"Mom…."

"Plus, you needed time to recover from your divorce. Just like he did from his."

I stayed silent, allowing her to continue.

"But now, seeing how good you two are with each other, I'm officially Team Matt. You light up around him. He's crazy about you. Knowing how much he cares about you — it warms my heart."

The tears I'd been holding back finally slipped through.

"He deserves honesty and transparency from you, Sarah. You can't hold back. Not anymore."

She let go of my hands, reached into her purse, and handed me a tissue. "Blow your nose, dear."

I did as told — loudly — then said, "This little talk of ours has brought back memories."

"Of?"

"Of me being a stubborn teenager. And you being the patient mother of a stubborn teenager."

"Oh, you weren't that bad," she said loyally.

"Yes, I was."

"Okay, fine. You definitely had your moments."

The two of us gazed at each other for a long moment.

"I'm so lucky to have you as my mom."

She blushed. "I'm the lucky one. You're a wonderful daughter."

"Most of the time?"

She laughed. "Yes, most of the time."

My attention shifted to Gabby, who'd remained remarkably silent.

Sensing that the need for statue imitation had

come to an end, Gabby gave Mom an approving nod. "Good job, Nancy. Tough love. I like it."

"Thank you, Gabby."

Gabby leaned forward and glared at me. "So listen to your mother for a change."

I smiled. "Got it."

"You managed to snag one of the good ones."

"I know."

Her glare intensified. "So stop acting like a dunce and get back on his good side."

"Got it."

"Because you've gotta spring him."

"Spring him?" I repeated, not following.

"The old crank. He really botched it."

I began to see. "You mean Mr. Benson."

Gabby's expression darkened. "Who else could be that stupid?"

"And you think —"

"Sarah, you're the only one who can save him." In her voice was the fear and concern she was trying so hard to hide. "He's not tough enough for the clink. He's a helpless lamb. He won't last a day. Those cons will tear him limb from limb."

"I'm sure Matt and his deputies are taking good care of him," I said, trying to reassure her.

"You have no idea what it's like in there. You have to rescue him."

I was about to respond when I heard a knock at

the cafe's front door. Mom and Gabby looked past me and froze.

I swiveled around —

And gulped when I saw Matt staring at us through the locked door.

As if operating in unison, Mom and Gabby immediately scooted out of the booth.

"You know what to do, Sarah," Gabby said as she dashed to the hallway door. "Get the old crank back home, pronto."

Mom unlocked the front door and let Matt in, then slipped past him. "Call me later, dear."

And with that they were gone.

Leaving me alone with the man I'd kept out of the loop. The man whose dark brown eyes were gazing at me with wariness instead of their usual warmth.

He looked so tall and powerful as he strode toward me, his broad shoulders straining this uniform, his jaw tight with tension, every inch of him the sheriff he'd become.

"Hey," I said meekly.

He slid into the booth opposite me, his expression serious. For a long moment he stared at me, silent and still. Then I heard the words I wanted and needed to hear, yet also dreaded:

"Sarah, we need to talk."

CHAPTER 23

He looked so solemn sitting across from me —
so focused, so handsome, so sincere. Yet also
… what was the word I was after?

Yes, *vulnerable*. I'd hurt him by withholding
something so important. And he was trying not to
show it.

I cleared my throat. "I want to explain."

"Please do." Though anger simmered in his
eyes, his voice was even. He wasn't ready to
forgive me — not even close — but he was here
and he was listening. For the moment, that was
enough.

"I found out Emily was alive last fall, the day
after Claire and I caught Amy," I said, referring to
the stone-cold assassin who had murdered two
people in my basement and nearly killed me as well.
"You'll remember the day. You and I were talking

letter sounds like her. But it turns out she didn't write it."

"Emily told you that?"

"That's why I had to go to Mom's house. To ask Emily."

"Why your mom's house?"

"Emily's agency did tech stuff to the computer at Mom's house so that Mom can talk securely with Emily."

"What did Emily tell you?"

"She didn't write the letter. Someone else did. Someone who knows Emily and her handwriting."

"When and how did Donald get the letter?"

"This morning. A stranger handed it to him at the flower show."

"What did the letter say?"

I showed him the fuzzy photo and read the letter out loud. He listened intently. I could almost hear the gears whirling in his head.

"Okay," he said. "Let's review what we know. The letter-writer is familiar with the scene of the crime and knows enough about the professor's death to provide Mr. Benson with a scenario for an accidental poisoning that, on the surface at least, is plausible."

"Right."

"Which means he — it could be she, but for now I'll go with he — was most likely in the tent at the opening reception."

"Agree."

"He also knows Polly is her mother's primary caregiver."

"Right."

"And knows Donald and Polly are friendly."

"Right."

"He also knows Donald and Emily were friends."

"Right."

"In theory, the letter-writer could have learned all of that from conversation and observation at the flower show. By spending time with Donald and Polly, for example."

"In theory, yes."

"Which brings us to Emily."

My stomach knotted. *Emily, whose survival we kept from him.* "Go on."

"The letter-writer knows Emily was once a spy and worked with Polly."

"Right."

"And knows Emily well enough to be able to write the kind of letter that Emily would write, with handwriting that closely resembles Emily's."

"Right."

"Which means he's a skilled forger or knows one."

"Right."

"All of which suggests the letter-writer is also a spy or former spy, or working with one."

"Right."

He took a deep breath. "But it appears the letter-writer doesn't know Emily is alive."

I hadn't considered that point yet. "Why do you say that?"

"Let's assume that the letter-writer's goal is to slow down the investigation. To distract us. Confuse us."

"Right." He'd used the word *us* — was that a good sign?

"If the letter-writer knows Emily is alive, then he knows the first thing we'll do when the letter surfaces is ask her if she wrote it. He'll know we'll quickly find out we're dealing with a fake. That's a lot of trouble to go to for at most a few hours of delay and confusion."

"But if the letter-writer believes Emily is dead...."

"Then he believes we won't be able to confirm the letter's authenticity quickly or easily. He thinks we won't be sure what we're dealing with. He thinks we'll have to consider every possibility, including whether Emily is still alive."

"And if we're looking at every possibility, then inevitably we'll be wasting time and resources...."

"Which is the letter-writer's goal."

"Okay, all of that sounds right. So that's the working theory. The letter-writer doesn't know Emily is alive."

"Just like me until an hour ago."

Oh, boy. He'd gone there. His gaze was intense, his jaw tight with tension.

"Matt," I began.

"Sarah, we're going to talk about that. But not now. First we have to catch a killer."

He glanced at his watch and slid out of the booth.

"Where are you going?"

"The station. A million things to do. The mayor is arranging background briefings with the media. The governor is demanding constant updates. It'll be another long night. I'll send Claire a photograph of Donald's letter — a good photograph."

"Matt, I'm sorry," I said as he headed to the door. "I should have told you sooner. I'm really, truly sorry."

He paused before leaving, his expression as intense as his tone. "Make no mistake, Sarah. When this is over, we're going to talk about that. We're going to talk about *everything*."

CHAPTER 24

With Matt's words echoing in my mind, I finished closing up the cafe and headed upstairs, every step up a chore. The never-ending whipsaw turns of the day had wrung me out.

I had just reached the third floor when my phone buzzed. It was a text from Hialeah. "I owe you an explanation. Any chance you're available right now?"

My pulse quickened. Tired as I was, I'd welcome the distraction — and the information. "Sure," I texted back. "Want to come to my place?"

"Thank you. There in 10."

After letting myself into the apartment, I did a quick inspection to make sure everything was presentable, then plopped down in the rocker by the front window and let out a gigantic, soul-cleansing sigh.

Oh, what a day. Since the moment I woke up, I'd been going nonstop. My poor body ached all over and my poor brain was begging for rest. As for my heart —

It thumped in my chest as I flashed to the shock and hurt in Matt's eyes. Tears threatened.

He'll come around, I heard Emily say.

I pushed back the surge, hoping with all my heart that she was right.

I gazed down at Main Street below, trying to will the tension away. The scene outside was quiet and dark, tranquil in its stillness.

A familiar baby-blue Cadillac DeVille rolled into view and slid into a parking spot across the street. Hialeah hurried across the street and buzzed to be let in. I rose from the rocker, crossed the living room, pressed the entry button on the wall next to the kitchen, then went to the apartment door and opened it.

I heard the soft rustle of her long dress and the gentle tap of her sandals on the hallway stairs before I saw the vibrant flash of her red hair. "Sarah," she said as she reached the third floor. "Thank you for agreeing to see me."

"I'm glad you've come," I said as I ushered her in.

She looked around with curiosity as she stepped into the living room, her attention drawn to Aunt Emily's wall of travel photos. She'd been in the apartment a few times, but most of our interactions had taken place in the cafe. We'd gotten to know each other fairly well in the six months since her arrival in Eagle Cove — certainly well enough for me to appreciate her basic kindness and decency. But she was a new friend — someone I needed and wanted to know better.

"Would you like some tea?"

She hesitated. "If it's not too much trouble?"

"No trouble at all." I zipped into the kitchen, filled the kettle, and set it on the stove. "Your usual? Earl Grey, splash of cream, dash of sugar?"

"Thank you."

As I got a tea tray ready, by unspoken agreement we steered clear of the topic that had brought her here. She asked about Emily's travel photos — most of them taken decades earlier when Emily and her husband Ted had traveled the globe — and my childhood years in Eagle Cove.

The kettle whistled. I poured steaming water into the teapot and set the pot on the tray. "Let's go into the living room."

"Can I help?"

"All good." I gestured toward the couch. "Make yourself comfortable."

As she sat down, adjusting her gown beneath her, I set the tray down and poured hot tea into two mugs. I watched her add cream and sugar to hers, then did the same and settled into my chair. "I'm glad you're here."

She took a sip. "After the way I behaved this afternoon, I knew I needed to explain."

This afternoon. The words sounded wrong. So much had happened in the four hours since Hialeah had fled in panic from the cafe.

"I'm all ears. Start wherever you like."

She took a deep breath. "How did you know I knew Professor Greeley?"

"I didn't, at least not for sure. But I noticed a couple of things. The morning the professor showed up, you were at your table getting ready for your first client of the day. A few minutes later, when I came downstairs to get the professor's trunk, you were nowhere to be seen."

She looked at me ruefully. "I ran away. The other thing?"

"The following day, when the professor was insulting everyone in the cafe, you saw him through the window and hurried off."

"I did, yes."

"I wasn't planning on saying anything. But when Mr. Benson made his big announcement, everything changed. I knew I needed to know the deal."

Hialeah sighed. "Professor Greeley and I crossed paths ten years ago in New Orleans. His wife came to me at a difficult moment in her life.

The professor was cheating on her. She wanted out of the marriage but was afraid to move forward. With guidance from the spirits, I helped her find the courage to escape."

My brow furrowed. "You helped the professor's wife figure out how to divorce him?"

"The spirits were the ones offering the guidance — her grandmother, to be precise — but yes, I facilitated."

Someday I was going to have to delve more into Hialeah's spirit world — everything she'd just shared was completely fascinating. But right now I needed to focus on the realm of the living. "And the professor…?"

"When he found out his wife was consulting me, he came to the tea shop where I did my readings and blamed me for the divorce. He said his wife was confused. He said I was preying on her. He called me a charlatan and much worse."

Her cheeks flushed. The pain the memory caused her was palpable.

"I'm sorry. That must have been awful."

"For all of the reasons you can imagine."

"So what happened then?"

"After the divorce, I hoped his anger would fade. But it never did. He continued to say things — cruel, unfair things — about me."

"You know that because you heard him or…?"

She shook her head. "New Orleans is a big city,

but in many ways it's like a small town. The community is tight-knit. Families and friendships go back generations. People talk. When Professor Greeley disparaged me, I found out." She shook her head sadly. "He had so much anger inside him. His aura was dark. His anger attracted malevolent spirits. They fueled him even as they twisted him."

I resisted the temptation to dig into that. "Thank you for telling me how you knew him in New Orleans. Is it okay if we turn to what happened here in Eagle Cove?"

She swallowed. "You want to know if I had any run-ins with him."

"Yes."

"For two days, I managed to avoid him. But he recognized me that first morning in the cafe. Two mornings later, there was a knock at my door and I opened it to find him."

I gasped. "He tracked you down? Thursday morning, before the reception?"

"That's right."

"That must have been frightening. What did he want?"

"I was afraid he was going to confront me about the divorce, but he didn't."

"What was he there for?"

"He wasn't angry. He seemed almost happy to see me."

I blinked with surprise. "Happy?"

"Like he was pleased to find me in Eagle Cove. Not because he enjoyed my company, but because...."

"Because you could help him with a goal of his?"

"Yes," she said. "That's how it felt."

"What did he want?"

"He wanted to talk about Eagle Cove — who I knew, what I thought about different people."

The professor was gathering research, I realized — asking about folks as part of his espionage assignment. "Which people?"

"He was interested in anyone who had lived in Eagle Cove for a long time."

"A long time? How long?"

"Decades, it seemed. He had a list of names."

"Who was on the list?"

She rattled off a bunch of names, including Mom, Mayor Johnson, Mr. Benson, Gabby, and Gabby's pals.

"What did he want to know about?"

"Financial difficulties. Infidelities. Substance abuse."

I frowned. The stuff he'd been asking about were things that made one susceptible to influence or blackmail.

"Anything else?"

"He asked about storage lockers and safe

deposit boxes. Where to rent one, who had one, that kind of thing."

"Any sense of why?"

Hialeah shrugged. "Perhaps he had something valuable with him and wanted to protect it?"

Or maybe he was looking for something valuable, I didn't say.

"Anything else?"

"He was in a hurry. As soon as he got what he could from me, he left."

In silent agreement, we refilled our mugs. What Hialeah had shared was intriguing.

I brought my mug to my lips, breathing in the comforting aroma. "Did you see him at the reception?"

"Yes, but we didn't speak." Then she added, "Though I noticed he seemed...."

"What?"

"Excited. Satisfied. Like a cat who'd cornered a bird."

"Unlike earlier?"

"Earlier he'd seemed impatient. Like he was still hunting."

He'd found something, I realized. A fact, a clue, a tidbit of information.

But what?

"If I'm remembering right," I said, "you didn't drink iced tea at the reception."

"That's right."

"What do you remember about the professor at the reception?"

"The sheriff and his deputies asked the same question. The professor arrived at the reception with the other judges at about one-thirty. They set their things down at the judges' table."

"What happened then?"

"About fifteen minutes later, I noticed Professor Greeley sitting alone at the judges' table, sipping from his teacup."

"Which means he was alive at one-forty-five. And then?"

She looked at me uncomfortably. "A few minutes after two, you kind of … barreled through the crowd. You seemed…."

"Drunk?"

"Yes. Sorry."

"No need to apologize. I was flying high. I just need to know what you saw."

"You managed to drag someone with you to the judges' table. That's when people began realizing he was dead."

Her account tallied with my disjointed recollections. "So tell me…. Who do you think is responsible for all of this?"

Hialeah shook her head. "I've asked the spirits. All they say is that the killer is hidden."

"Hidden? What does that mean?"

"I'm sorry, that's all I can tell you."

I was about to ask her more when my phone buzzed. I picked it up and saw it was Deputy Martinez.

"Sorry, I need to get this." I brought the phone to my ear. "Hello, Deputy. How can I help you?"

"Ms. Boone, glad I reached you. The sheriff has asked me to gather Professor Greeley's belongings and bring them to the station. Could I use your dolly to get the steamer trunk down the stairs?"

"Of course," I said. "Are you here?"

"Yes, I'm parked outside."

"I'll be right down." After hanging up, I turned to Hialeah. "I'm sorry, the deputy needs my help moving something…."

"Of course," Hialeah said, rising to her feet. "Thank you for giving me the opportunity to explain."

"I'm glad you did. Thank you for trusting me."

"The spirits are glad you're here, Sarah. They have a name for you."

"They do?" I said, surprised.

"They call you 'the Necessary Woman.'"

I felt myself flush. "They call me *what?*"

"It's a good thing." Her brow furrowed. "At least, I think."

"Um, then I guess you can tell them I said … thank you?"

We left the apartment and I followed her down

the stairs, noting again the quiet rustle of her gown as she moved.

"Thank you again, Sarah," she said when we reached the sidewalk. "See you tomorrow?"

"See you tomorrow." As she hurried across the street to her car, Deputy Martinez hopped out of her truck, which was parked in front of the cafe.

"Come on in," I told her, holding open the entry door. "The dolly's in the cafe."

She followed me inside. After retrieving the dolly from the cafe storeroom, I lugged it up the stairs to the studio apartment and unlocked the door.

"Let's roll the dolly inside and get it as close to the trunk as we can."

The steamer trunk was exactly where it had been yesterday afternoon at the foot of the bed. Together we lifted it onto its side, slid the dolly under it, and then rolled it out of the apartment.

"Now we need to make sure it stays steady as we bring it down the steps."

It was only as we were making our slow descent, one bumpy step at a time, that I sensed something was off.

At first I couldn't pinpoint what. Then I realized — the trunk seemed heavier.

When we reached the bottom of the stairs, I almost didn't say anything. The two of us took a second to catch our breath, relieved we'd made it down without a spill.

"You know," I said apologetically, "I almost hate bringing this up, but the trunk feels different."

The deputy said, "What feels different?"

"It's heavier than when I lugged it up the stairs a few days ago."

She frowned. "That's unlikely."

"I think we should check it."

"You mean, open it?"

"Yes."

"Right now?"

"Yes."

"That's not proper procedure."

"Still…. Better safe than sorry, right?"

I don't know what convinced her — I'm betting on a combination of her natural thoroughness mixed with a dash of human curiosity. With a resigned sigh, she helped me maneuver the trunk off the dolly and onto the floor.

With me looking over her shoulder, Deputy Martinez pressed the latch and lifted the lid.

And I heard myself gasp with horror.

Staring up at us from inside the trunk, her sightless eyes filled with blood —

Was Polly Pence!

CHAPTER 25

I hadn't expected to find a dead body, I swear. Yes, the trunk seemed heavier and I was curious why — but that's as far as my brain got before Deputy Martinez opened the lid and shocked me to my core.

For those of you keeping track, Polly was the fifth corpse I'd discovered in seven months. Prior experience did *not* make the moment easier. Though I barely knew Polly, I liked and respected her. Her death saddens me still.

After a few seconds of stunned silence, Deputy Martinez shut the lid, sat me down on the stairs, called Matt to report in what we'd found, and examined me for signs of shock. Then she took out her notebook and began taking my statement. Matt arrived a few minutes later, followed by Doc Barnes and the crime scene techs, and I found myself swept

up once again in a police investigation. At some
point Gabby poked her head out of her apartment,
alerted by the noise. "You gonna blame the old
crank for this one, too?" she snarled at Matt. "A
maniac is killing flower show judges and you locked
up an innocent man!"

During the long slog of the next few hours, the
investigative team devoted most of their attention to
the studio apartment and the steamer trunk, but
every inch of the building got searched yet again. I
did my best to be helpful by making pot after pot of
coffee for the army swarming the scene.

Barely thirty minutes after we found the body,
my phone started exploding, starting with a call
from Mom, whose first words were, "*Another* dead
body, Sarah? Really?" Over the next two hours, I
fielded a flurry of calls and texts from Janie, Claire,
Mayor Johnson, and Edgar. I was also bombarded
with texts and calls from Wendy and her media
colleagues, all of which I firmly ignored.

Finally, as midnight neared, the investigators
wrapped up their work and headed out. I was in the
cafe's kitchen, washing the coffee pot and
wondering if Eagle Cove's rollercoaster ride of
death would ever end, when Matt appeared at the
kitchen door.

"Hey," he said quietly.

"Hey."

He looked bone-tired. Two dead bodies in three

days will do that. In his hand was a clear plastic bag with a sheet of paper inside it. "Something you need to see."

"What's that?"

"She left a suicide note."

I breathed in sharply. *What the…?*

"It was inside her jeans pocket." Carefully, he laid the letter on the prep island's stainless-steel countertop.

Heart pounding, I leaned down and read:

Sheriff Forsyth,

This note is my confession. I killed Beauregard Greeley and drugged the iced tea at the reception.

I didn't mean to kill Beauregard — I meant to incapacitate him. But I'm not sorry he's dead. We had a history. He was a terrible man. The world is better off without him.

As for getting everyone high without their knowledge — I deeply regret that. Getting stoned is one of life's great joys, but so is consent. I hope the good people of Eagle Cove can find it in their hearts to forgive me.

I also wrote a letter, delivered to Donald Benson, in which I blamed myself for Beauregard's death. I wrote the letter in haste, when I still believed I had a way out of this mess, and I hired a courier service to hand-deliver it to Donald. I hope you and Donald will accept my apology for trying to fool you so clumsily.

I'm choosing to end my life to protect my mother. Her

health is frail. I do not want her final years filled with worry, heartache, and shame, which is what my trial and imprisonment would bring. Also, I have no desire to spend my remaining years behind bars.

I beg you — please tell my mother I passed quickly and without pain. Tell her I was in good spirits on my final day. Tell her I spent my last hours with the flowers I love. Tell my brother I have every confidence he will be a wonderful caregiver.

You'll wonder why I chose to hide myself in Beauregard's steamer trunk. I'm afraid I don't have a good reason for that — the idea came to me and I can't seem to let it go. I suppose I'm curious how long it will take for you to find me. Revenge might be a factor as well — Beauregard was always so fastidious about his possessions. He'd hate having his precious trunk sullied in such a manner.

You'll also wonder how I shut the latch on the trunk from the inside. When you investigate this question, you'll discover that doing so is quite possible. The only person involved in my death was me.

Sincerely,

Polly Pence

P.S. Mom and Brian — I love you both. I'm so very, very sorry.

I looked up, astonished. "This letter is…."

He nodded. "I know."

Desperately, I tried to wrap my head around

what I'd just read. "About the trunk. Is the letter right? Is it possible to latch it from the inside?"

He took another plastic bag from his pocket.

The bag looked empty until I squinted and saw a piece of thread. "What's that?"

"This," he said with a sigh, "is the thread Polly had in her hand. If you take the thread and loop it through the latch on the trunk and pull it…."

I gaped at him, incredulous. "You can actually close the latch from the inside of the trunk and then pull the thread inside the trunk?"

"The crime scene techs just showed me how."

"Wow." I said, now even more flummoxed. "What about the handwriting? Is it Polly's?"

"Don't know yet. We showed part of the letter to Harriet. She wasn't sure. We've asked Polly's brother to send us a sample of her handwriting."

From the deeply unsatisfied look on his face, I knew exactly what he was thinking. "Your expectation is that the handwriting will match Polly's."

"Yes."

"You expect that because Mr. Benson's Emily letter was a really good forgery."

"Yes."

"Which means you're wondering if the Polly letter is fake, too."

"The thought had crossed my mind."

"At the same time," I barreled on, "you're

wondering whether the fake Emily letter was written by Polly, and whether that means the Polly letter is the real deal."

"Yes."

"It's also possible, of course, that Polly forged the Emily letter and someone else forged the Polly letter."

He shrugged. "Also possible."

It was then I realized why he was sharing all of this with me. "You want me to ask Emily if Polly's skill set included forgery."

"I left a message with Claire but haven't heard back."

I thought back to the afternoon convo in Mom's kitchen — a meeting that seemed like it happened ages ago.

"Polly came up in discussion today at Mom's house."

"How so?"

"I asked Emily if Polly really worked for H.U.S.H. and whether they'd known each other. Emily said she did but that they'd overlapped only briefly."

"Anything about Polly having forgery skills?"

I shook my head. "The only thing Emily knew was that Polly worked as a researcher, not an agent. Claire said she'd find out more."

He sighed. "I'll wait for her call."

"How is Harriet, by the way?"

He grimaced. "Shocked, shaken, grieving, afraid. She and Polly were old friends."

"Is she in danger?"

Something — worry? — flashed in his eyes. "Could be. I've assigned a deputy to protect her. Just in case."

At that moment, another figure appeared at the kitchen door: Claire.

"Hey," she said. "Got here as fast as I could. What's the latest?"

I pointed to the letter on the table. "There."

She stepped closer and started reading, her expression darkening as she absorbed what the letter said.

"I assume this was on the body?" she asked.

"Yep," Matt said.

"And appears to be genuine?"

"Yep."

"But might also be a good fake?"

"Yep."

"I got your voicemail," she said to Matt. "No, Polly's file did not list forgery as one of her skills."

"Which doesn't mean she didn't do this."

"Right."

For a long moment, the three of us were silent.

"There are two possibilities here," I finally said. "If the suicide note is the real deal, then Polly killed the professor, poisoned the reception guests, forged the fake Emily letter, and killed herself after realizing she wasn't going to get away it."

"The story's a good one," Matt said, "if the suicide note is real."

"Right," I said. "So this will sound a bit odd, but stick with me for a minute. I was chatting with Hialeah earlier. She told me the spirits shared with her that —"

"Wait," Claire said. "We're getting intel from *ghosts* now?"

"Well, kind of, but let me explain, okay?"

Claire's expression conveyed quite clearly her opinion about the reliability and value of information obtained from the so-called spirit world, but to her credit she managed to keep her trap shut.

"She said the spirits were telling her the killer is 'hidden,' which in and of itself doesn't mean much. But it got me thinking. What might the killer be hiding behind?"

"No idea," Claire said. "A rock? A tree?"

That's when I asked the question I'd been pondering for the past hour or so.

"No," Claire said immediately. "We checked."

"Can you check again?" Then I asked my next question.

"That's a leap," Claire said.

"But can you check? If only to rule out the possibility?"

With a sigh, she brought her phone to her ear and relayed my requests.

"One more thing," I added. "Something Polly said yesterday."

"What did she say?"

I told her, then added, "I think that means —"

"On that I agree. It does lend itself to what you're guessing at."

Matt was watching us thoughtfully. "It would explain a lot."

"It would," Claire said.

Her phone buzzed. She looked at it and her jaw dropped.

"You're not gonna believe this, but...."

And then she told us.

Matt's eyes widened and I felt faint with shock at actually being right.

"We need to confirm all this," Claire said. "I mean, really dig in."

"Of course," I said.

"As for what to do right now, the easiest path is for us to swoop in."

"You mean H.U.S.H.?" I asked.

"Yes."

I shook my head. "If you do that, the town will never know who did it. We need an arrest. We need a win. Eagle Cove deserves to see justice served."

"Sarah's right," Matt said.

"I sympathize," Claire said, "but how do you plan to accomplish that? You have no proof."

I was about to open my mouth to protest when I realized she was right.

Claire turned to Matt. "Do you even have enough for a search warrant?"

He shook his head. "Not even close."

"I want the same thing you do. But unless we can come up with a plan — right here, right now — I need to have H.U.S.H. intervene. The risks are too high."

"A plan?" I said. "That's all we need? That's easy. We can come up with a plan."

"Just like that? The three of us? Snap our fingers and — voila?"

"Well," I said slowly, hoping to buy my brain enough time to glom onto something – anything — that might actually work. "You say the problem is there's no proof."

A smile played at Matt's lips. "You're saying…."

"What if we create the proof?"

Claire regarded me for a long moment, clearly torn. Part of her, I knew, wanted to kick me out of the room so that the professionals could do their jobs without the distraction of a certain meddlesome, nosy amateur. But another part of her wanted to see what her pesky pal might come up with.

"I can't believe I'm saying this," she finally said. "What do you have in mind?"

"Well…."

And that's how it started. I told them my idea and the three of us spent the next two hours refining it — arguing over it, challenging it, tweaking it. There were moments in our back-and-forth that reminded me of high school, back when everything we did felt fresh, vital, and exciting. Inevitably, however, the importance of getting it right added weight to our task and kept us tethered to earth.

Finally, when we thought we were ready, Claire whipped out her laptop and brought the plan to Emily for her review.

"Are you sure about this?" Emily asked after listening carefully.

"I don't see any other way," I said.

"Claire? Matt?"

Matt shrugged. "It's our best shot."

Claire said, "If it works, great. If it doesn't, we can still…."

Emily's mouth tightened. She wasn't pleased. "I had hoped to keep you separate from this terrible business, Sarah."

"I know."

"Yet here you are, in the thick of it."

"I'm sorry about that."

"You're not sorry at all."

She was right, of course. Undaunted, I held her penetrating gaze.

"A great deal is riding on you."

"I know."

"As plans go, this confection you've whipped up is gossamer-thin and fantastical. It depends on people who know nothing about the plan following a plan they know nothing about."

"I know."

She stared at me for a long moment through the computer screen. "Very well," she finally said. "Be careful. Godspeed."

And we were off.

CHAPTER 26

A few minutes after eight on Sunday morning, I drove to the sheriff's station to set in motion a chain of events that Claire and Matt and I knew had very little chance of playing out as we hoped.

Nevertheless, despite the extremely low odds of success, we were determined to try. For Eagle Cove's sake, we needed to give this our best shot.

At the station, I found Deputy Martinez at the front desk. The main room was empty and quiet.

"Holding down the fort?"

The deputy nodded. She'd had a very long night and looked completely beat. "The sheriff ordered everyone else home for four hours of sleep."

"And you?"

She shrugged. "Short straw. Next shift."

"It's been a long four days. Hopefully this will be over soon."

"The sheriff texted. He said you'd be here for…..?"

"That's right."

She stood up. "Back in a minute."

While waiting, I reached into my handbag and nervously fingered the sealed envelope I was carrying. Inside the envelope was a letter from Emily for Mr. Benson. But unlike the first Emily letter, this one was the real deal.

I heard a door open and looked up to see the deputy leading Mr. Benson from the back. At Matt's request, he'd spent the night at the station, bunking in an empty jail cell. Though his clothes were rumpled, he seemed alert and focused.

"Good morning, Sarah," he said.

I greeted him with a smile. "How are you feeling, Mr. Jailbird?"

"I slept well, all things considered. Deputy Martinez and her colleagues were very kind."

The phone rang at the front desk. "Excuse me," the deputy said.

I turned my full attention to Mr. Benson, swallowing a stab of anxiety. It's one thing to dream up a ridiculous idea in the dead of night, but quite another to stare the reality of it in the face.

No way around it — this was going to be tricky. There were so many pieces to this convoluted puzzle. So many players. So many layers. So many lies that needed to be told, just so.

A lot was riding on Mr. Benson, though he didn't know it.

"I have something for you," I said quietly as I handed him the letter. "I found it slipped under my door thirty minutes ago." I lowered my voice to a whisper. "I have to know — is it from you-know-who?"

After glancing at Deputy Martinez to make sure she was still busy on the phone, Mr. Benson opened the envelope and started reading the words that Matt, Claire, and I had helped Emily write:

Donald,

Change of plans. I have arranged for Sarah to hand-deliver this letter to you. She doesn't know who wrote this letter and will be curious and persistent in her quest to find out, as is her nature. Tell her the letter is from a prospective attorney. When she asks you to share it with her, gently but firmly tell her no.

Whatever you do, you must not tell her I am alive. Sharing my secret could place her and you in danger. If by chance you've already confided in her about my first letter, I must ask you to backtrack. Tell her that after further reflection, you no longer believe I am alive. Tell her you believe the first letter was a prank. Tell her you're perturbed that someone would go to such lengths to hinder the investigation into Professor Greeley's murder.

I'm writing because I must ask you to complete an additional, extremely vital task. I cannot share why this task is so important and for that I am sorry. When I see you next — a moment I look forward to — I promise I will explain all.

You will soon be released from custody. The instant you are free, you must take Sarah with you to meet with the remaining flower show judge, Harriet Vale.

You need to warn Harriet and Sarah that they are both in danger. I repeat: When you go to Harriet, you must take Sarah with you. Sarah cannot be left alone today. Do not let her out of your sight, even for a moment.

When you and Sarah meet with Harriet, tell them you believe Professor Greeley was killed because of something that may be hidden in Sarah's building.

Explain that the former owner of the building — do not mention my name — kept a lot of secrets. Tell them I had a knack for hiding valuables in odd, unexpected places. Tell them I'd once given you a framed picture and, in the frame, hidden a key to my apartment. Tell them I enjoyed giving gifts to friends that contained concealed compartments and the like.

Tell Harriet and Sarah you're sharing this information to warn them that they're in danger. Tell them Professor Greeley was looking for something and asking everyone in town about safe deposit boxes. Tell them your apartment was broken into and searched on Friday.

Tell Sarah she's in danger because the building belongs to her. Tell Harriet she's in danger because the killer may believe Greeley confided in her or entrusted her with something for safekeeping. Tell them Polly Pence's death convinced you of the need to warn them.

Your friendship means the world to me, Donald.

When I see you next, I promise I will explain everything.

With much love and appreciation,

Emily

Mr. Benson looked up from the letter, clearly stunned.

"Who's the letter from?" I whispered. "Is it from you-know-who?"

He flushed. "No one," he stammered. "I mean, a lawyer. Not Emily."

"What did the lawyer say?"

"Nothing." He paused to collect himself. "I mean, nothing important. A legal matter. Nothing to worry about. Would you excuse me?" Then he dashed to the restroom.

"Of course," I said innocently as I watched him hurry away.

He stayed in the bathroom a good ten minutes — long enough to read the letter several times and collect his thoughts.

Finally he emerged, the letter safely tucked in his coat pocket, his composure restored. "Thank you, Sarah. I appreciate you waiting for me. Would you mind if we take a detour before returning home?"

"Sure, no prob," I said as we left the station and headed to my SUV. "But come on, tell me about the letter. I'm dying here."

"The method of delivery does seem mysterious, but I assure you it's from a lawyer. A legal matter that I'd prefer to not discuss at present."

"Really?"

"Yes, Sarah. Really."

"Okay, if you say so," I said, acting disappointed. "Where to?"

"I would like to check in on Harriet. After what happened with Polly, I feel terribly for her."

"Of course. That's very thoughtful of you. I can only imagine how upset she must be."

"She's staying at Elmer and Maddie's."

We climbed into the SUV and turned toward the Eagle Cove Inn, a charming Victorian bed-and-breakfast a few blocks off Main Street run by a local married couple, Elmer and Maddie.

In the passenger seat, Mr. Benson cleared his throat. "I had time in my jail cell last night to reflect upon the letter I shared with you yesterday."

"Oh, you did?"

"I've come to the conclusion that it was a cruel prank."

"A prank?" I said, acting surprised.

"Someone — who, I do not know — took advantage of my sadness over Emily's death."

I pretended to be skeptical. "Why would they do that?"

"I believe the letter is an attempt to obstruct the investigation into Professor Greeley's death."

"Oh, I see," I said, trying to sound taken aback. "Now that you mention it, that makes sense. Who would do that?"

"I have no idea."

"So … are you saying Emily isn't actually alive?"

"I would love for her to still be with us. Unfortunately, I no longer believe that to be the case."

I let out a disappointed sigh. "I'm sure you're right. The idea was so improbable anyway."

"Agreed. It's best to forget the letter exists."

"Forget? Are you sure?"

"I am," he said firmly. "The sheriff has enough on his plate already. We must not complicate his investigation further."

CHAPTER 27

So far, so good — Mr. Benson was following Emily's script admirably. With a tiny flame of hope in my heart, I pulled in front of the Eagle Cove Inn. Even among our town's abundance of Victorian-era beauties, the Inn is truly a standout. Built in the late 1800s as a single-family mansion for a wealthy lumber merchant, the building had been transformed by Elmer and Maddie into a popular bed-and-breakfast establishment. Painted in a crisp nautical white with blue and gold trim, it oozed Georgian-style charm.

Mr. Benson and I made our way across the lawn, up onto the beautiful wraparound porch, pushed open the oak front door, and stepped into the front parlor. From the direction of the dining room we heard the clink of silverware. We followed the sound and found Harriet at the table, staring blankly at a cup of tea and a half-eaten piece of toast. Standing nearby was Deputy Paul, who'd been assigned to protect her.

Harriet was looking — I'll go ahead and say it — rough. Her face was pale and drawn, her face puffy with grief. Beneath her heavy black wool coat, she was dressed in a dark blue blouse and black slacks.

She didn't notice us at first. When she did, she stiffened.

"I'm sorry," she said. "You startled me."

"It's we who should apologize," I said immediately. "We didn't mean to surprise you."

"It's not your fault. I'm just … jumpy."

Mr. Benson took the chair next to her. "Harriet, I am so terribly sorry about Polly. Please accept my deepest condolences."

She gazed at him, her eyes bright with tears. "Thank you, Donald. You're a dear man. And — you're out of jail. They let you out."

"Yes, just now."

"It was so silly of them to suspect you of anything."

"I appreciate you saying that."

Anxiety flashed across her face. "Why are you here? Has something else happened?"

"No, no, nothing like that." Mr. Benson threw me a glance. "There's something I need to share with you and Sarah."

"Share with *us?*" I said, acting puzzled.

"Yes, both of you." He turned to Deputy Paul. "Deputy, could I ask you to step away for a few moments? I need to have a private conversation with Harriet and Sarah."

Deputy Paul blinked. "Um, okay, I guess? I can do a perimeter check. I'll be right outside if you need me."

"Thank you."

After watching him leave the dining room, Mr. Benson gestured to a chair next to Harriet. "Have a seat, Sarah."

I sat down as requested. "What's going on, Mr. Benson?"

He gazed at us with solemn resolve. "I have had time to reflect upon the terrible events of the past few days. I believe I understand the nature of what has occurred. When I heard the terrible news about Polly, I realized I had to warn you both right away."

Harriet and I exchanged surprised glances.

"Warn us?" I said. "About what?"

"I believe both of your lives may be in danger."

"*What?*" I exclaimed.

Harriet's face grew paler. "Why do you say that, Donald?"

"I will do my best to explain." He glanced at me. "I'm sorry, Sarah, but this involves your aunt."

"My aunt?"

"As you know, she and I were friends for more

than thirty years. Over time, I came to understand certain things about her."

"Okay…."

"She was, of course, a wonderful, generous, thoughtful woman. She was also quite fond of secrets. Not gossip — that's not what I mean. Rather, secrets of the physical sort. She had a knack for hiding things in odd, unexpected places."

I furrowed my brow, as if not convinced. "She did?"

"For example, she once gave me a framed photograph. In the frame was a secret compartment in which she'd hidden a key to her apartment."

"Oh, I see. I didn't realize she did that with everyone, but sure, that rings a bell. Back when I was a kid she gave me a little jewelry box with a hidden drawer. I thought it was the greatest thing ever. But what does that have to do with what's going on?"

"I ask that you bear with me as I explain." He turned to Harriet. "When Sarah's aunt died, Sarah inherited her building."

"I assume you're referring to the building with the cafe on the ground floor?"

"Yes," he replied. "I live on the second floor and Sarah lives on the third. The reason I've mentioned Sarah's aunt and her enjoyment of secrecy is that I believe something is hidden in the building."

"Hidden?" I said, acting puzzled. "In the building?"

"I believe Professor Greeley was looking for it. I also believe the professor's killer is looking for it."

"Wait," I said, acting confused. "*What?*"

"It's the most reasonable explanation for the events of the past week."

I shook my head. "I am totally *not* following."

Harriet chimed in. "Donald, I'm sorry, but I'm with Sarah on this."

"Yeah," I added, "you have to unpack that. Start with Professor Greeley. What does he have to do with this?"

"I'll do my best to explain," Mr. Benson said. "Before he died, Professor Greeley was asking around town about safe deposit boxes."

I blinked. "He was?"

"Then, the day after someone killed him, someone searched my apartment."

Harriet stiffened. "Your apartment was searched?"

"On Friday afternoon, while we were all at the flower show."

"Was anything taken?"

He shook his head. "The only reason I know is because items were moved."

"Why would someone do that?" Harriet asked.

He shrugged. "Clearly, they were after something."

Harriet looked dubious. "Something that Sarah's aunt hid there?"

"Yes, exactly."

I let out a sigh. "How about — just for grins — we play along with this theory of yours. The professor was looking for something, and now the killer is looking for it."

Harriet frowned. "Sarah, do you believe that's what happened?"

"No. I'm not there, at least not yet."

"I see. Go on."

"Let's say my aunt hid something somewhere and the professor was looking for it and now the killer is looking for it. What in the world would that something be?"

Mr. Benson shook his head. "I'm sorry, I don't know."

"I mean, I can't imagine anything in our town being of even the slightest interest to Professor Greeley. He hated everything about Eagle Cove."

Mr. Benson shrugged. "I can't answer your question, Sarah. There is much we don't know about...." He hesitated, as if weighing how much to reveal. "About the past."

I rubbed my forehead. "This is giving me a headache. It's way too early in the day for this. I haven't even had my morning latte."

Harriet said quietly, "Donald, why are you sharing this with us?"

"I believe this object — I will refer to it as such without knowing what it is — has placed both of you in danger."

Harriet frowned. "Why?"

"In your case, Harriet, because you and Professor Greeley were both judging the show. The killer may believe the professor confided in you or entrusted you with something."

"He didn't," she said right away. "That didn't happen. Beauregard and I were not close, Donald."

"The killer may not know that. As for you, Sarah, I'm even more worried about you."

I breathed in sharply. "Why?"

"Your aunt's building belongs to you now. Someone broke in on Friday. And now, with poor Polly dying there under such mysterious circumstances...."

"It wasn't mysterious," I said. "It was suicide."

Harriet let out a gasp. "Suicide?"

"Oh, gosh," I said immediately. "I'm so sorry. I shouldn't have said anything. I only know because I was there. Please accept my sincere apologies."

"Suicide?" Harriet repeated, her voice filled with horror.

"There was a note."

"A *note*? Is that why they asked about her handwriting?"

"The sheriff's investigating. We'll know more soon."

Harriet was shaking her head. "What could possibly drive her to…."

"I know this is a delicate topic," Mr. Benson said, "but I may be able to shed some light."

"How?" I said, secretly a tad alarmed. Polly wasn't part of the script that Emily had given him in her letter — what was he about to say?

He took a deep breath. "I believe it's possible that Polly was involved in Professor Greeley's death."

"*What?*" I exclaimed, hoping he wasn't going to bring up the first (fake) Emily letter.

He seemed to realize his mistake, because the next thing he said was, "I'm afraid I can't say more. In fact, I may have said too much."

"Donald," Harriet said, "you can't make a claim like that and not back it up."

"I apologize," Mr. Benson said. "You're absolutely right. To be clear, what I said is pure speculation. Still, I can't help but wonder whether Polly's desire to avoid Professor Greeley may have led her to act rashly."

"Rashly? In what way?"

"I would hate to compound my error with additional speculation."

"You know," I said with what I hoped was the right amount of skepticism and strained patience. "This, um, theory of yours — it's an awful lot to take in."

"Yes, it is," Mr. Benson conceded.

"But to summarize, what it boils down to is, you want me and Harriet to be careful."

"Yes. If my theory is correct, then both of you are at risk. I wouldn't want anything to happen to either of you."

Harriet shook her head. "I appreciate you saying that, Donald. I don't know if I agree with your theory, but I will admit I'm glad to have Deputy Wilkerson with me."

"I'm glad you have him, too. As for you, Sarah, you have me."

I blinked. "What?"

"I'll be accompanying you today. At your side at all times."

"That's very kind of you, but it's not necessary."

"All the same, I shall."

I smiled. "My very own bodyguard? How very gallant."

Harriet rose to her feet. "If you'll excuse me, I'm going to return to my room. I didn't sleep well last night. I should try to rest."

"Of course," I said. "Will we see you later?"

"Mayor Johnson has asked me to announce the winners at the awards show. I didn't want to, given everything that's occurred, but your mayor is … very persuasive."

"She's definitely that."

"Will you please tell Deputy Wilkerson I went upstairs and will be resting?"

"Of course."

"Thank you both for coming here." She turned to Mr. Benson. "Donald, I appreciate your thoughtfulness and concern. I can see why Polly was so pleased to make your acquaintance."

CHAPTER 28

Sure enough, for the rest of the day, Mr. Benson stuck to me like glue.

After saying goodbye to Harriet, we left the Inn and returned to our apartments to briefly freshen up before heading down to the cafe, where Janie was busy baking muffins and other assorted treats for delivery. After boxing up the muffins, Mr. Benson and I drove the boxes to the Eagle Cove Common and carried them to the media tent, where a horde of hungry journalists descended upon us and quickly consumed every single one.

"It's like they haven't eaten in weeks," I said, marveling at the ferocity of their hunger.

"You're going to need a lot more muffins," Mr. Benson said.

"On it," I said, whipping out my phone to text Janie.

We ended up making two more round trips that morning and a final one that afternoon, with Mr. Benson an eager participant every step of the way. He really was a dear, sweet, generous man. Though he believed he was protecting me, the truth of the matter was the opposite: Keeping him at my side was intended to protect *him*. It was possible the killer had concerns about what Polly might have shared with him. The last thing Claire, Matt, and I wanted was to give the killer the opportunity to tie up that loose end.

After the frantic pace of the previous night, the day seemed to move like molasses. Mr. Benson and I did our best to keep busy with muffin deliveries, and we also helped Mom and her volunteers set up the reception tent for the awards ceremony.

Inevitably, however, there was down time that allowed doubts to creep in. The previous night, fueled by adrenaline and caffeine, the plan that Claire and Matt and I had come up with seemed bold but plausible. But now, in the bright light of day, I realized Emily was right: Our confection was impossibly thin. If a single ingredient didn't get added in the exact right way, the town would never see justice served.

A jolt of hope arrived mid-morning with a text from Claire. "Bait taken. We're on."

My pulse jumped. One ingredient added, a

thousand to go. Was it possible our ridiculous little gambit might actually work?

I looked up from my phone and found Mr. Benson watching me. "Sarah, is something wrong?"

"Oh, nothing," I said hastily, stuffing my phone into my pocket. "Thinking about the awards ceremony."

"I'm glad the mayor decided to move forward. The people of Eagle Cove need something good to cheer about."

"Totally agree. What do you think of your chances? Does your orchid have a shot at winning?"

He shook his head. "Unlikely. The competition this year was very strong."

"Well, I wish you the best of luck."

"Thank you."

Finally, as the late afternoon sun began casting shadows across the Common, the time arrived for the Eagle Cove Flower Show's closing ceremony. In the reception tent, rows of seats had been arranged facing the raised stage at the end of the tent. A big "Eagle Cove Flower Show" banner hung behind the stage.

Throughout the tent, final preparations were under way. On stage, Mom was fiddling with the microphone on the lectern and a volunteer was setting a water glass and a pitcher of iced tea on the panelist table next to the lectern. In the back of the tent, Edgar was busy helping set up a row of TV cameras as the reporters jostled for position. With so many media types in town hungry for news, our little awards show was getting the star treatment.

The crowd began flowing in to claim their seats, Mayor Johnson and Harriet among them. The mayor looked tired but determined, her gaze sweeping the tent in search of problems to solve. Harriet, still in her black-and-blue ensemble, looked a bit more composed than she had this morning, though her face remained pale.

I greeted them as they approached. "Harriet, were you able to squeeze in a nap?"

"Thankfully, yes. Every little bit helps."

"Glad to hear."

"Mrs. Vale," the mayor said, "thank you again for agreeing to judge our show and for presenting today's awards. I appreciate how difficult this is for you. The entire town is grateful."

"You're welcome, Mayor Johnson."

The mayor glanced at the TV cameras. "I need to make sure our friends in the media are being well cared for. If you'll excuse me...."

As she stepped away, I said to Harriet, "So what's on the program today?"

"Thankfully, it's short. The mayor will open the ceremony and I will hand out the awards."

"And then it's over?"

"Yes. And finally this terrible weekend will come to a close."

I shivered. Terrible weekend indeed.

Mom bustled up. "Harriet, we've arranged a table and chair for you on stage."

"Thank you, Nancy."

"Sarah, I've saved a spot for you next to me. Front row."

"Thanks, Mom."

She looked at her watch. "Goodness. It's time."

After completing a final task, I took my seat in the front row next to Mom. Glancing behind me, I spotted Mr. Benson and Hialeah two rows back, with Gabby and her gaggle — Mrs. Chan, Mrs. Bunch, and Ms. Hollingsworth — one row behind.

Mr. Benson gave me a reassuring smile. "I'm right here."

"Thank you," I replied.

As I turned back around, I saw Matt position himself at the side of the tent, about halfway between the stage and the back. When his eyes found mine, he gave me a quick nod.

My stomach tightened, nervous energy bubbling up.

Fortunately, before unhelpful thoughts could take over and drive me too far down the all-too-familiar rabbit hole of soul-gripping dread, Mayor Johnson and Harriet stepped to the stage. Harriet took her seat at the table and poured herself a glass of iced tea as the mayor took the lectern. "Ladies and gentlemen," she said, her voice as quietly commanding as always, "please take your seats. We're ready to begin."

After a short wait to allow stragglers to squeeze into the last available seats — the tent was packed — the mayor began her remarks. I will confess I don't remember what she said. I'm sure her words were eloquent and appropriate. My brain was fully occupied by visions of impending doom as the ridiculous stunt I'd so eagerly pushed for us to attempt drew ever-nearer.

I remember the mayor introducing Harriet and thanking her for judging our flower show despite the difficulty of the circumstances. And I remember Harriet rising to her feet as the audience applauded and, after a sip of iced tea to clear her throat, taking the lectern.

"Thank you, everyone," she said as the audience quieted down. "I have served as a judge at dozens of flower shows over the past quarter century. It's fair to say I have never judged a show like this one."

She took a deep breath to steady herself, then continued.

"My two fellow judges, Beauregard Greeley and Polly Pence, are no longer with us. Four days ago they were both here, and now — they're not. Beauregard was highly regarded for his expertise, and Polly" — she swallowed back emotion — "was not only a brilliant researcher and scientist, but a dear friend. I can't believe I no longer have her in my life."

The audience remained silent, their sympathy for her clear.

"After hearing the terrible news last night about Polly, the last thing I expected to do today was attend this ceremony. But Mayor Johnson prevailed upon me to reconsider. She reminded me how important it is for us to honor not only the beautiful flowers that drew us here, but those we have lost. It is in this spirit, in memory of those no longer with us, that I announce the winning entries in this year's competition."

She removed a sheet of paper from her coat pocket and adjusted her spectacles. "We will begin with the Specialty classes. I will be announcing the winners only. The second- and third-place results will be posted on the website after the ceremony. I would like each winner to stand briefly when her or his name is announced and for the audience to applaud briefly. In the African Violet class, the winner is…."

And so it began. With more than two dozen competition categories, the reading of the names took a while, but a rhythm quickly developed. Harriet announced a winner, the winner stood up, the audience clapped for a few seconds, and Harriet announced the next winner. Her experience with crowd-handling became clear as she kept the announcements moving forward briskly.

Finally, she said, "Ladies and gentlemen, we've saved the best for last. I'm pleased to present the grand prize of the Eagle Cove Flower Show, the coveted Golden Pot, awarded to the entry deemed the year's most worthy."

Next to me, Mom reached under her seat, grabbed this year's Golden Pot, and brought it to the stage. Though not much to look at — it's just a small, unremarkable flower pot painted in gold — the Golden Pot's importance to the audience was clear in the way everyone tensed and stirred.

Harriet accepted the pot from Mom and turned back to the microphone. "This year's winner is a flower that in my experience is often overlooked. This specimen impressed both Polly and me with its exquisite form, proportions, and coloring. Despite its petite size, it possesses a quiet strength that sets it apart. In our many years of judging, it's one of the most stunning examples of its species we've come across."

She paused dramatically and held the Golden Pot in front of her. "The winner is: The Lady Hillingdon tea rose grown by Wilhemina Chan!"

The audience erupted in applause and Mrs. Chan cried out with delight. Gabby, Mrs. Bunch, and Ms. Hollingsworth rose to their feet, hooting and hollering as Mrs. Chan made her way to the stage to accept her award.

Mayor Johnson rose from her seat at the table and joined Harriet at the lectern. "Congratulations to all of this year's winners. Harriet, thank you again for judging this year's show."

She turned to the audience. "Before concluding today's ceremony, we have one more speaker. Please, everyone, remain seated for a few more moments."

Puzzled, the audience began murmuring amongst themselves. When Harriet looked inquiringly at the mayor, the mayor gestured for her to return to her seat at the table.

"Citizens of Eagle Cove," the mayor said, her voice carrying effortlessly over the crowded tent. "Before we disperse, one of our own would like to share her thoughts about the terrible events of the past few days."

In my seat in the front row, I felt my stomach lurch. Even though I'd known this moment was coming, terror stabbed through me. *Oh geez oh geez oh geez, why oh why oh why had I agreed to do this?*

"Without further ado," the mayor said, "please welcome to the stage — Ms. Sarah Boone."

CHAPTER 29

Shakily, I rose from my seat and made my way onto the stage, my stomach doing somersaults and my heart pounding away like a jackhammer.

When I reached the lectern, Mayor Johnson stepped from the stage and took my seat in the audience next to Mom. From her seat at the table next to me, Harriet looked at me, puzzled and curious.

I gripped the lectern to steady myself and turned my attention to the audience. A sea of faces, row after row of them — endless and vast, seemingly extending into eternity — gazed at me, waiting for me to open my mouth and say something interesting and informative. Behind them, a bank of TV news cameras aimed their lenses my way, ready to capture — for posterity, oh my! — whatever foolishness might tumble from my mouth.

My stomach lurched. I wanted to throw up. Was I making a huge mistake?

"Thank you, Mayor Johnson," I said, alarmed by the tremble in my voice. *Buck up*, I ordered myself.

From her seat in the third row, Hialeah smiled encouragingly. *You can do this*, she seemed to be telling me. *The spirits are with you.*

I cleared my throat. "I know everyone is eager to congratulate Mrs. Chan and the other winners for their well-deserved victories. But first, I'd like to speak with you for a few moments about the terrible events of the past few days."

From the audience came murmurs. In the front row, Mom glanced sharply at Mayor Johnson, who avoided Mom's gaze and kept her focus firmly on me.

Forgive me, Mom, I silently implored her. *I knew you'd object to what I'm about to do and there was no way to tell you with Wendy stuck to you like a barnacle, so I decided to keep you out of the loop.*

"I'd like to begin by saying I would much rather *not* be standing here. What I'm about to share is difficult and painful."

More anxiety flooded through me — I tried to push it back. "I'm here because Eagle Cove has endured the unthinkable. A killer is in our midst. And justice must be served.

"The mayhem we experienced at this year's flower show hit very close to home for many of us. It certainly did for me. Professor Beauregard Greeley was murdered in this very tent, a few feet from where I stand now, at a reception that *my* cafe catered. The person who discovered him dead was *me*.

"Make no mistake — my involvement in this case, my presence on this stage today, is totally, completely the fault of the person who committed this terrible crime."

I took a deep breath. The audience was quiet. I sensed their sympathy and interest. "I want us, as a community, to be able to move forward from what happened. To do that, we need to confront it. We need to understand it. We need to *solve* it."

The audience stirred. *Solve it? Does she mean…?*

"I'm here today to tell you who murdered Professor Beauregard Greeley."

I heard gasps. Now I definitely had their interest.

"Here's what's going to happen. First, I'm going to tell you who *didn't* commit the crime. After that, I'm going to reveal the identity of the murderer. I'll also tell you how the killer did it and why."

It was in that moment that I realized two things:

The audience was with me. And I no longer felt like throwing up.

"I'll begin with a prediction. I predict the killer will surrender to the sheriff, right here in this tent, in just a few minutes."

More whispers came as the audience looked over at Matt and back at me and wondered — *How can she know that? Has the poor thing lost it? Should someone intervene and gently escort her off the stage?*

From the front row, Mom was vibrating with alarm. *Sarah*, she was practically screaming without words, w*hat in the world are you doing?*

"So let's get started by talking about who *didn't* do it. If you've read this morning's *Gazette* or watched the news" — I gestured toward the row of TV cameras — "then you know that a dear friend of mine, Donald Benson, was questioned yesterday in connection with Professor Greeley's death."

From his seat in the third row next to Hialeah, Mr. Benson nodded encouragingly.

"Mr. Benson believed he was involved because, a few moments before the professor died, he prepared a cup of tea for the professor. He believed the sugar might have been poisoned by someone. As a responsible citizen, he felt it was his duty to share his suspicions with Sheriff Forsyth."

Folks in the audience had realized that Mr. Benson was here and were gawking and whispering.

"Fortunately for Mr. Benson," I said above the

whispers, "it turns out the sugar *wasn't* the source of the poison used to kill Professor Greeley. I'm very pleased to report that Mr. Benson had *nothing* to do with the professor's death. I'm sure Sheriff Forsyth will be happy to confirm this."

From his spot at the side of the tent, Matt said loudly, "Confirmed."

"Thank you, Sheriff."

From the audience, Gabby gave me a big thumbs-up.

"Now, I'd also like to discuss the rumors swirling around another friend of mine, Ms. Hialeah Truegood."

In her seat, Hialeah flushed pink and nodded for me to continue.

"All of us in Eagle Cove know the ins and outs of rumors. We are rumor *experts*. We know how they get started and we know how they spread. We also know how important it is for us to dispel *unfounded* rumors. After all, we want our facts to be right.

"So here's the full, unvarnished truth about Ms. Truegood and Professor Greeley. As many of you know, both are from New Orleans. Their paths crossed there once, briefly, many years ago, when the professor's wife was a psychic client of Ms. Truegood's."

After giving the audience a few seconds to absorb that, I continued. "Professor Greeley was unhappy about his wife consulting with Ms.

Truegood. He confronted Ms. Truegood in a public setting in New Orleans — in a tea shop — and demanded that she stop working with his wife. Beyond that encounter, the two of them had zero interactions — zero — before the professor arrived in Eagle Cove on Tuesday."

I paused again to make sure the audience was with me — they were. "The professor's arrival in Eagle Cove surprised Ms. Truegood. She made every effort to avoid him. But on Thursday morning, a few hours before the flower show reception, he showed up unannounced at her door. Ms. Truegood was afraid he might still be upset with her, but it turns out he was pleased to see a familiar face. The two of them chatted briefly about Eagle Cove. They then parted ways.

"And that, ladies and gentlemen, is the sum total of Ms. Truegood's interactions with Professor Greeley." I gestured toward Hialeah in the audience. "In her short time with us in Eagle Cove, I've grown quite fond of Hialeah. I value her counsel and support. I know I speak for many of you when I say we're lucky to have her."

Hialeah flushed even pinker.

"That's why it's so important for all of us to help set the record straight. Ms. Truegood had zero involvement in Professor Greeley's death. I repeat — zero. I'm hoping the sheriff can confirm that."

From his spot at the side of the stage, Matt said loudly, "Zero."

"Thank you, Sheriff," I said.

The audience swung their attention back to me. They were getting the hang of what I was doing — bringing up a suspect, then clearing him or her.

"Now I'd like to say a few words about one of our flower show judges, Polly Pence. As many of you know, Ms. Pence was found dead last night. The investigation into her death is ongoing. I believe Sheriff Forsyth is preparing a statement about the status of that investigation for his press conference later this evening."

When Matt gave me another nod, I continued.

"There is one point about Ms. Pence that I can clear up right away. There's a rumor going around — I've heard it and so have many of you — that Ms. Pence and Professor Greeley were once an item. That rumor is true." I waited for the murmurs to grow and subside. "Twenty-three years ago, for a brief time, they dated — until Ms. Pence learned that Professor Greeley was married and ended the relationship."

The audience glanced at each other, clearly wondering if I was building up to a big reveal about Polly.

"Those who knew Polly well" — I cast a sympathetic glance at Harriet seated onstage next to me — "knew that she did not like or trust

Professor Greeley. When she learned that Professor Greeley was here in Eagle Cove, she wasn't happy about him being here."

I waited to let all that sink in. "I know what you're all thinking. It's a fair question, one that needs to be asked. Was Polly Pence's unhappy history with Beauregard Greeley motive enough for her to kill him?

"I wondered the same. For a brief moment, she was my top suspect. Love and hate can be powerful motivators."

I gestured toward Matt. "The Sheriff has given me his okay to share that he and his deputies have investigated Ms. Pence's possible involvement thoroughly, in particular her movements on the day the professor was murdered.

"The question they asked was: Did Ms. Pence have the *opportunity* to kill Professor Greeley? Was there a moment in her busy day when she could have done it?"

I took a deep breath.

"The answer to that question, it turns out, is no. Polly Pence had *zero* opportunity to poison the professor's tea. In fact, as soon as she and her fellow judges arrived at the reception, Ms. Pence went to the opposite side of the tent and remained there without interruption. As I'm sure the sheriff will confirm, Polly Pence did *not* kill Professor Greeley."

"Confirmed," Matt said.

"Thank you, Sheriff." I surveyed the audience to make sure they were with me — they were. "So let's recap. We've cleared three possible suspects. Now it's time to turn to who did it.

"As the sheriff announced on Friday, Professor Greeley was poisoned. The state lab has determined that the poison is a type of plant alkaloid. The lab is doing additional toxicological analysis to identify the specific plant. Sheriff, am I describing the poison correctly so far?"

"Yes," Matt said. "Your description is correct."

"During his press update yesterday, the sheriff shared two important pieces of information about the poison. One, it was found in the professor's teapot. Two, it's extremely fast-acting. Within minutes of drinking the poisoned tea, Professor Greeley was dead.

"The pot of tea was prepared moments before it was given to the professor. That means the individual who added the poison to the professor's tea did so in a crowded tent in front of dozens of potential witnesses. It takes a lot of — I'm trying to come up with a word that doesn't sound complimentary — *nerve* to risk that. This individual lessened that risk by dumping a hallucinogenic substance and a bunch of sleeping pills into the iced tea that everyone was drinking.

"The killer's gamble almost paid off. Professor Greeley died. Dozens of reception attendees

— myself included — drank the iced tea and ended up too stoned or sleepy to remember anything of value to the sheriff and his team.

"You'll note I said 'almost.' The killer made a mistake. A tiny mistake. Perhaps what you'd consider an ironic mistake, given that we're gathered together here this weekend to celebrate the power of flowers."

The audience looked at me, puzzled and a tad impatient. *There's nothing ironic in anything you just said, Sarah. Please stop dilly-dallying.*

"The killer's mistake was a small flower. A beautiful lily — an Orange Pixie Lily — entered into the competition by my dear friend, Ms. Gabby McBride."

In her seat next to Mr. Benson, Gabby did something she rarely did: She blushed.

"The killer should have known better, too. I mean, the killer is an expert, a true expert, when it comes to all things floral. Hence the irony. Isn't that right, Harriet?"

I turned toward Harriet, who was sitting next to me on the stage.

She looked up at me, her brow crinkling in confusion. "I'm sorry, is what right?"

"I'm right about the irony of the killer being brought down by a flower. After all, the killer is a renowned flower expert. A horticulturist of impeccable reputation. A judge of flower competitions far and wide, including right here in Eagle Cove."

Harriet's eyes widened. From the audience, I heard shocked gasps.

"Sarah, what are you saying?"

"What I'm saying, Harriet Vale, is that Beauregard Greeley was murdered by *you*."

CHAPTER 30

Harriet gaped at me in utter astonishment. "What did you say?" she said, her shock carrying effortlessly over the hushed audience.

"It brings me no pleasure to be standing here in front of everyone and identifying you as the killer," I said, relieved to hear my voice remaining steady. "I'd prefer to be pretty much anywhere else, doing anything else. But you heard me loud and clear. The person who murdered Professor Greeley is *you*."

Harriet's face conveyed a perfect mix of confusion and hurt. "Sarah, I did no such thing."

"You put lethal poison in Professor Greeley's tea and dumped a hallucinogen and a sedative into the iced tea. In doing so, you killed your fellow judge and endangered the health and safety of a hundred people."

"I assure you, I did none of that." She looked toward Matt. "Sheriff, what is the meaning of this?"

Matt shrugged. "Looks like Sarah has more to say."

The audience was eagerly taking all of this in — every word, every gesture. And while I sensed their fascination, I knew they wouldn't be satisfied until they heard more — a lot more. All I'd done so far was lob accusations. Did I have any proof?

"You know," I said, looking right at Harriet. "Blackmail is such a dangerous thing. Someone discovers your secrets and threatens to expose everything you've worked so hard to hide. With so much at stake, what is one to do?"

A flush rose on Harriet's cheeks. I'd scored a hit.

"What I'm trying to say is, I get why you did it. Every decision you made, every action you took, I get. I mean, in no way do I *agree* with what you did — what you did makes you a complete and total monster and I hope you spend the rest of your life rotting in prison — but I get it. For example, I know why you went to the main tent this morning and smashed that flowerpot."

Harriet blinked with surprise. "What are you talking about?"

"I'm talking about pot smashing, of the secret sort."

Her puzzled expression was superb. "I did not smash any pot."

"Oh, but you did. This morning, when you thought no one was looking, you went to the main tent and grabbed a flowerpot. You hid the flowerpot in the folds of your coat — the same big black coat you're wearing right now — and left the tent. Then you took the pot to a quiet spot and smashed it to pieces."

"Sarah, I —"

"The flowerpot you smashed is the same one you and I talked about on Friday. I'm sure you recall. The pot was a bit on the chunky side and painted in vibrant colors."

"I'm afraid I recall no such conversation."

My pulse quickened. She'd made her first mistake — a tiny one, granted, but it gave me an opening.

"Really? You don't recall our conversation from just two days ago?"

Harriet paused, trying to decide how to respond.

"Hey," I said before she could reply, "the good news here is that you forgetting all about a conversation that took place just two days ago is actually totally okay, because guess what? I remember our conversation very clearly and so does Donald Benson, who was there as well." I gestured to Mr. Benson in the third row. "It is of course quite sad that the fourth person in that conversation, Polly Pence, is now very conveniently dead."

Murmurs arose from the audience at my mention of Polly.

Harriet had realized I was trying to undermine her credibility and she knew how to read a room. "Sarah," she said, her voice firm and clear, "I'm trying to be patient with you. Everyone in Eagle Cove has been through a terrible ordeal, including me. I don't recall the conversation you say we had, but even if we did have it, how can it possibly matter?"

"It matters because you smashed the flowerpot we were talking about."

"Again, I did not do that."

"Oh, but you did. In fact, there's proof. Visible for all to see."

Harriet's eyes widened with astonishment. "Proof? Visible?" I had to give it to her — her acting was superb. "My dear, I don't know what to say."

"As a horticulturist, you're well aware that a defining characteristic of lilies is their pollen, which adheres to any surface it comes into contact with."

She went still — I'd surprised her.

"Pollen from a lily can be extremely hard to get off fabric. When it's smeared on, it sticks."

"I have no idea what you're implying."

"If you'd like, we can settle the matter right now. Please stand up and hold your arms out."

She blinked, taken aback. "Why would I do that?"

"Do you have something to hide?"

"Of course not."

"Then let us — all of us — get a look at your coat."

She sat still for a moment, deliberating. She had options, after all. Her safest path would be to tell me to stuff it — to rise to her feet and march off in a huff. If she chose to not play along, there was basically nothing I could do to stop her.

But I was banking on her curiosity and fear winning out. Harriet was comfortable with risk. Her maneuvers this weekend proved that. She knew I had a plan of my own but didn't know what it was. Given everything she'd already done, she'd feel compelled to find out what I had up my sleeve.

Still acting thoroughly bewildered, she glanced down at her coat.

"Very well," she said, her tone a perfect blend of reluctance and uncertainty.

She stood and gave the audience a puzzled shrug.

"Thank you, Harriet. Would you mind slowly turning around and raising your arms?"

She almost objected but chose to go along. "Very well."

As she twirled, we all saw it: a stain of orange

on the underside of the left sleeve of her coat, bright and visible against the dark fabric.

"There," I said, pointing to the stain. "That's it."

Murmurs arose from the audience. They saw the stain — but what did it mean?

"As a friend recently told me," I said, "the stain reveals."

In her seat in the audience, Hialeah smiled.

"Reveals what?" Harriet said. "I have no idea what this is or how it got there."

"I'm sure you recognize that stain."

"I'm sure I don't."

"It's pollen from the lily in the pot you smashed."

She pulled the sleeve closer to examine it. "I didn't smash a pot."

"The stain wasn't on your coat yesterday."

"You can't know that."

"Oh, we can and do. It turns out there's video of you from late yesterday afternoon." I gestured toward Edgar and his ever-present camera. "The flower show hired an excellent videographer. He's super-thorough. He got a great shot of you leaving the main tent late yesterday afternoon. And guess what we found when we reviewed the footage? No stain."

Harriet peered at Edgar as if thoroughly perplexed. But her jaw tightened. Perhaps that was the moment she realized Edgar was no ordinary event videographer.

"So now we get to the importance of the stain on your coat. I mean, why do we care about a stain? And what's so special about a flowerpot?"

Harriet went still as she realized what was coming next.

"What matters is what was *in* the flowerpot. Something hidden. Something secret."

Harriet changed her expression to puzzled. "I have no idea what you're talking about."

Neither do we, I could hear the audience thinking. *Stop being so vague. Give us some proof!*

"What I'm talking about," I said, "is a flash drive full of information. Hidden in the flowerpot."

The audience didn't know what to make of that. *Flash drive? Information? What kind of information?*

"You've gone mad," Harriet said as she picked up her handbag and prepared to leave. "I'm done humoring you. Your accusations are baseless and painful."

"It's like I said earlier. Blackmail is a terrible thing. I can only imagine what's on that flash drive."

Shaking her head with disapproval, Harriet turned to address the audience. "I'm sorry everyone had to witness this. Your friend has gone off the deep end."

"Tell me, Harriet," I said, undeterred, "when

the sheriff arrests you, is he going to find the flash drive in your possession?"

"He is not going to arrest me," she said right away. "He has no grounds to arrest me."

"What if I told you that, in addition to video of you yesterday with a stain-free coat, there's video from this morning of you smashing the flowerpot?"

"I'd say you were lying," Harriet snapped.

"Ah, but what if I'm not?"

Harriet's gaze darted to Edgar, who gave her a shrug. "Sorry, lady. She asked me to be on the lookout for you, so...."

I went in for the kill. "You're holding your handbag very tightly, Harriet. I wonder why. You planning to make a run for it? Maybe because the flash drive from the

flowerpot is in your handbag? Tell me I'm right. You have it. It's on you. The flash drive is in your possession."

Harriet flushed, her eyes burning holes into me. "Flash drives — you can get them anywhere."

"That's true in the general sense," I replied. "But a flash drive with my fingerprint on it?"

As my words sank in, gasps rose from the audience.

Harriet's nostrils flared. "You set me up."

"Totally," I said immediately.

She hadn't expected me to admit that. She

glared at me, her mind racing. And then — I could see it happening — she realized something.

"Even if what you're saying about the fingerprint is true," she said slowly, "the only thing that might prove is that I broke a flowerpot and found a flash drive."

The crowd swung their attention to me, riveted. It was like a TV crime drama unfolding in real life.

Harriet had a point. Did I have a worthy response?

In the back of the tent, I found Claire. She shook her head and held up a finger.

Stall, she was saying. *One more minute.*

"The way I see it, you have a choice." Inspiration struck at the sight of Harriet's half-empty glass of iced tea. *Could I? Should I?*

Before I could stop myself, I plowed forward. "And by 'choice' I mean the choice of who you talk to."

Harriet frowned, not following. I couldn't blame her — I was barely following either.

"Who you choose to talk to is so important," I continued. "And why you talk, of course. And by why, I mean what's influencing you."

Now I had her thoroughly confused. The audience, too.

"I mean, think about all the lovely flowers entered into this year's competition," I said brightly. "So beautiful. Their power over us

— their ability to persuade and influence — is undeniable."

Harriet's eyes narrowed — she'd realized my babble had a purpose.

"Such beauty, such power. They can make one feel so different. In my case, when I'm under their influence, I feel lighter, more buoyant, more expressive."

Harriet's gaze darted to the iced tea. Oh, yes — she was following me. And wondering — *had the tea been dosed with the orchid hallucinogen?*

"You know, it's not just me," I said cheerfully. "Flowers affect everyone. Friends can meet up and, if there's a nice bouquet of flowers at the table, they'll find themselves opening up, relaxing, expressing themselves in ways they never would normally. Flowers encourage us to socialize and share."

Harriet's nostrils flared.

In the back, I caught movement. A man in a dark suit — a total secret agent type — had joined Claire. He was about our age, with sharply defined features and slicked-back blond hair.

Claire gave me a nod.

When I turned back to Harriet, I found her staring at Claire and the man. Bright spots of color rose in her cheeks.

"Now of course," I added helpfully, "there's also the timing aspect of all this. I mean, we know flowers are at their most impactful when they're fresh. Their effects can last for hours before fading."

From the crowd, I heard murmurs of concern. *Why all the babble about flowers? Has poor Sarah lost it?*

"That's why who you choose to be with when flowers are fresh is so important. I mean, I know who I'd rather spend my time with." I gestured to Matt at the side of the stage. "But everyone is different. The choices we make about who we spend our time with are so important, especially when it comes to sharing our hopes and dreams."

Harriet swiveled toward me.

"Especially when those dreams involve our loved ones."

At my words, she went completely still.

"Our loved ones mean so much to us, don't they? In moments like this, who you choose to socialize with can make all the difference, not just for you, but for them."

And then I went quiet. And waited.

In the long seconds that followed, anger flashed in Harriet's eyes, but also calculation.

This was it — her moment of decision.

She breathed in deeply and exhaled. And then, her mind made up, she turned to Matt.

"Sheriff, I would like to confess to breaking the flowerpot and taking the flash drive."

Gasps arose from the audience.

Matt shook his head. "That's not enough, Mrs. Vale."

The flush on Harriet's cheeks deepened. After an excruciating pause, she said, "I also confess to the accidental death of Beauregard Greeley."

As soon as the magic words left her mouth, the audience erupted. Cries of astonishment rose in the air. *She'd just confessed!*

Harriet said, "Sheriff, I will not say another word until I speak with my attorney."

Matt stepped to the stage, cuffs in hand, his demeanor serious and professional.

But as he read Harriet her rights and led her out of the tent, I knew exactly what he was feeling, because I was feeling the exact same thing:

Huge relief mixed with amazement that our highly improbable plan had actually worked!

CHAPTER 31

The aftermath was pandemonium, of course. Half the audience rushed the stage, engulfing me in a cacophony of congratulations and questions.

Overwhelmed and alarmed, I was trying to figure out how to escape when Mayor Johnson barreled through the throng and spirited me away.

"Media tent," she said, gripping me firmly by the arm.

"Can't I take a minute to catch my breath?" I begged.

"Sorry, no time. They're closing in."

I looked over my shoulder and gulped — an army of rabid reporters was giving chase.

The instant we reached the media tent, Mayor Johnson stood me in front of a colorful "Eagle Cove

Flower Show" banner and switched on a bank of lights.

As I blinked under the sudden glare, Mayor Johnson turned to face down the baying media horde. "Ladies and gentlemen of the press," she said firmly, commanding them to silence with a stern look. "I've asked Ms. Boone to meet with you and she's agreed — but only if you behave. I expect each and every one of you to treat her with courtesy and respect. Five minutes for each reporter. The line forms to my left."

After a few seconds of stunned silence, the reporters scrambled into line. And so began a seemingly endless stream of interviews as reporter after reporter stuck microphones and TV cameras in my face, each of them eager for "exclusive" quotes and details for their stories.

The reporters already had the video footage of the awards ceremony, so most of their questions were follow-ups — how I'd figured it out, what I'd felt up there on stage, how it had been arranged, and so on. After the first few interviews, I started hearing the same questions and my answers became automatic:

"No, her confession didn't surprise me. Guilt is a heavy burden to bear."

"Fortunately, the clues were all there. I'm glad I was able to notice them."

"Yes, I felt very nervous up there on the stage,

but I knew something had to be done."

"No, I have no idea what secret she's worried about. You'll need to ask her."

"Yes, the mayor and the sheriff knew what I was going to do."

"I'm relieved it's over. Our town didn't deserve what we were put through. Everyone in Eagle Cove is ready to move forward."

"Thank you — I'm so glad you enjoyed the muffins. My cafe co-owner, Janie McKendrick, is an amazing baker. Next time you're here, be sure to swing by Emily's Eats in the heart of downtown Eagle Cove."

Finally, after ninety minutes of nonstop questions, the media horde had had its fill and dispersed, leaving one last reporter: Wendy from the *Gazette*.

"Nice job," she said, tipping an imaginary hat to Mayor Johnson.

"Thank you, Wendy," Mayor Johnson said.

"I mean, giving each reporter an 'exclusive' but rushing us along like widgets on a conveyer belt before any of us could even begin to unpack the crazy stunt you pulled? Seriously, kudos to you both."

"You're welcome to ask me any question you want, Wendy," I said evenly.

"I could, but what's the point? All I get from you is evasion."

"Well," I replied, aware she was trying to goad me. "I don't think that's fair. What you got from me today is a humdinger of a story."

Her gaze didn't waver. "But not the full story."

"Wendy, I —"

"Stop. Please. You know more than you're letting on. You know that. I know that. Pretending otherwise is an insult."

I shrugged. "Then I guess there's nothing more to say."

"And I guess today's not my lucky day." She checked her watch. "Okay, off to dutifully transcribe your boyfriend's highly edited version of reality."

Before I could pipe up in Matt's defense, she stormed away.

I took a deep breath, savoring the sudden silence. Dusk was slipping into night. The air was cool and still. In the exhibition tents, volunteers were busy breaking down tables and folding up chairs. At long last, the Eagle Cove Flower Show had come to a close.

Mayor Johnson reached for the plug for the lights illuminating the flower show banner. With a yank, the tent went dark.

"You did well today, Sarah. Thank you."

"I never want to talk to another reporter again," I said with a groan.

She chuckled. "You and me both."

As I adjusted to the semi-darkness, I glanced around the now-empty tent. "Where are Mom and Matt?"

"At the sheriff's station. His press conference starts in fifteen."

"If you need to get there…."

"I'm heading there now." She glanced around to make sure we were alone, then added, "Someday, Sarah, I hope you will tell me what's really going on."

I blinked with surprise. "Mayor Johnson, I…."

"That odd little flower soliloquy of yours — it had a point. Something you said convinced Harriet to confess."

I swallowed, trying to figure out how to respond.

She reached out and squeezed my hand. "No rush. In your own good time. Thank you again."

And then she was off.

As if waiting for her to leave — which was probably exactly what they were doing — Claire and Edgar emerged from the shadows.

"Congrats, Sarah," Edgar said with a big grin.

"Thank you. Did I do okay?"

"You did great. Confession through confusion — pretty advanced-level stuff."

"Honestly, I barely knew what I was doing. I almost got lost in my own blather."

Claire was smiling as well. "Your track record as

a spy-catcher continues unblemished."

"I'm relieved it went the way we hoped. It was touch-and-go until that secret agent guy arrived. Harriet recognized him. Who is he?"

Her smile faded. "A colleague."

"His presence frightened her."

When Claire didn't reply, a memory stirred.

"Wait. I've seen him before. Last fall at your family's farm, he was there in a big black SUV. The two of you were arguing."

She sighed. "He's the new boss."

"Acting boss," Edgar amended.

"I see." I stared at them for a few seconds. "So we don't like him."

Edgar tried to hold back another grin and Claire shook her head with irritation. "As we've discussed, there's no 'we' here. You need to keep from getting more involved in H.U.S.H. than you already are."

"Okay, fine. Message received. I've never seen Mr. Acting Boss, I don't know Mr. Acting Boss, and I don't need to pretend I don't dislike Mr. Acting Boss, even though that's how we all feel about him."

"You know," she said with a sigh, "I came here to thank you and congratulate you, not chastise you for your apparently inexhaustible, irrepressible, never-ending nosiness. Please stop forcing me to stomp all over what I was hoping would be our feel-good moment."

I held my arms out wide. "Deal."

She stepped in and gave me a big hug. "Thank you, Sarah," she said in my ear.

"You're welcome."

"You drive me batty sometimes."

"I know and I'm sorry."

"You're not even slightly sorry."

"That's probably very true."

As the hug ended, Edgar said, "On that note, I'm off. Duty calls. Sarah, as always, a pleasure."

"Will I be seeing you again soon?"

"Afraid so."

"Swing by the cafe anytime — coffee and muffin on the house."

"Count on it," he said with a grin, then vanished into the darkness.

I turned to Claire and sighed — because our day's work was not done.

"Longest Sunday ever," I said.

"Almost there." She glanced at her watch. "Matt's press conference starts in a few and will go forty-five minutes, maybe an hour."

"So … nine?"

"Sounds good."

I pulled out my phone and typed a group text to Gabby, Mr. Benson, Hialeah, Janie, Mom, Claire, and Matt.

"I have more to share," I texted. "Your ears only. My place at 9."

CHAPTER 32

Shortly before the appointed hour, the gang began arriving. Gabby and Mr. Benson showed up first, followed by Hialeah and Janie. With Claire's help, I got them settled in the living room with glasses of wine and tea. Mr. Snuggles clambered through the dumbwaiter shaft in the kitchen wall to join in the fun as well. After rubbing himself against everyone's legs, he hopped onto the sofa between Gabby and Mr. Benson and settled in like he owned the place, which was appropriate since he pretty much did.

Mom and Matt arrived last, direct from the sheriff's station.

"How'd the press conference go?" I asked as I ushered them into the foyer.

"It went fine," Matt said.

"Matt did great," Mom said. "It got pretty lively, but he handled it well."

"Lively?"

He shrugged. "There was bit of a pile-on at one point about letting a civilian lead the charge."

I frowned. "Let me guess. Wendy. She whipped her colleagues into a lather."

"Did she ever," Mom said. "The woman's on a tear."

I sighed. Part of me sympathized with Wendy's frustration. After all, she was right about me keeping tons of stuff from her. Still, I didn't like her taking out her annoyance on Matt.

Matt gestured toward the assembled crowd. "Can't stay for long. Shall we?"

"Let's."

We stepped into the living room, and Mom and Matt took the remaining empty seats.

"Everyone good?" I said. "Anyone need a refill?"

"All good, Sarah," Mr. Benson said.

For a brief second, I surveyed our little gang. From experience, I knew that a private chat with key gossipers would help cement in place the version of events that H.U.S.H. wanted Eagle Cove to believe was the truth.

The previous night, Claire and Matt and I had decided what we could and couldn't share.

Now it was time to implement that plan.

"Thank you for gathering on such short notice. Matt can't stay long, so let's dive right in. He's agreed to share additional information with you because each of you, in your own way, got caught up in this mess, and each of you deserves to know the full story. All we ask is that you keep to yourselves what we're about to share."

I expected no such thing, of course — I was counting on them blabbing every single juicy tidbit at lightning speed — but I gave them what I hoped was a solemn look and continued.

"First, I'm hoping Matt can update us on Harriet and her arrest."

Matt cleared his throat. "As you witnessed this afternoon, Harriet Vale publicly confessed to the accidental death of Beauregard Greeley. She's been arrested on suspicion of murder. She informed me she won't be saying more until she meets with her lawyer. He's due in town tomorrow."

"She's a slippery one," Gabby growled. "Watch out."

"We're taking no chances. Fortunately, thanks to her public confession and an array of physical evidence, we have an excellent case."

"What kind of evidence?"

"Sorry, I can't disclose those details yet."

Gabby frowned — she'd been hoping for something she could dig her teeth into — then swiveled to me. "Sarah, on stage today, you said Harriet broke my flowerpot on purpose."

"That's right," I replied. "She was looking for a flash drive."

"A flash drive with what on it?"

"Honestly, I have no idea. But whatever's on it is pretty important to her."

Mr. Benson spoke up. "You said you put the flash drive in Gabby's flowerpot?"

"That's right. Early this morning, before I picked you up at the station."

Janie looked puzzled. "And the stain on her coat?"

"I smeared it on her coat this afternoon, right before the awards ceremony."

Mr. Benson's frown deepened. "Wouldn't those actions be considered tampering with evidence?"

"Not at all. All I did was lie to her."

Gabby cackled with delight. "Good one, Sarah."

"But," Mr. Benson continued, "you manufactured evidence. If the authorities used that evidence to arrest her...."

"Ah, but they didn't. The stain and the flash drive aren't evidence."

Mr. Benson looked inquiringly at Matt, who said, "Sarah's correct. The stain wasn't on Harriet's coat until Sarah placed it there before the awards ceremony. I watched her do it. Same with the flash drive. Neither the flash drive nor the stain were factors in her arrest."

"Same with the video evidence," I added.

"What video evidence?" Mr. Benson said.

"Exactly. There was none."

"But you told her there was."

"Again, I lied. To get her to confess, we had to make her believe we had evidence."

Mr. Benson still wasn't convinced. "Why did she surrender so easily? She's a capable, resourceful individual. Surely she'd have the sense to keep quiet, hire a top attorney, and vigorously contest any charges."

His question was excellent. Unfortunately, I couldn't share the real reason — that she'd preferred to surrender to Matt rather than to H.U.S.H.

"Well," I said slowly, "I can't say what was in her head in that moment on the stage. Some people get flustered in front of crowds — I know I do. Perhaps she fell prey to her emotions?"

"Perhaps," Mr. Benson said slowly.

"Perhaps it's even simpler — she felt guilty about what she did."

"You mean, about killing Professor Greeley?" Hialeah said.

"No," I said, readying my first truth bomb of the evening. "I mean about killing Polly Pence."

The room gasped.

"Harriet killed Polly, too?" Janie said.

As planned, I glanced at Matt as if requesting permission, then said, "If I share something, you have to promise not to tell a soul."

"Of course," Janie said immediately.

"Not a soul," Gabby added, her eyes alive with anticipation.

"Our lips are sealed," Mr. Benson added.

From his spot on the sofa, Mr. Snuggles threw in an encouraging purr. *Come on, tell them. You know you want to....*

"Sarah," Matt said, as planned. "I'm not sure —"

"They deserve to know," I replied immediately, also as planned.

Matt let out a planned sigh of frustration, then gestured his assent.

In unison, Gabby, Mr. Benson, Hialeah, Janie, and Mom leaned forward.

After a suitably dramatic pause, I said, "You probably heard that Polly left a suicide note."

They glanced around, waiting for someone else to be the first to admit that yes, they knew all about it.

I didn't bother waiting. "There's good reason to believe the note was fake."

Everyone gasped.

"A fake suicide note?" Mom said. "How in the world…?"

Briefly, I summarized where the note was found and what it said.

Mr. Benson shook his head. "I must say, the note doesn't sound like Polly."

I gave him an encouraging look. "You knew her better than any of us. Why do you say that?"

"I don't believe she would have willingly or preemptively left her mother. The two of them were very close. They shared everything. If Polly had been arrested, her mother would have been upset, yes, but she also would have been Polly's fiercest defender. The fight would have energized her."

"Mothers will do anything for their children," Mom added.

"So what you're saying is that her stated reason for killing herself…."

"Doesn't align with what we knew about her," Mr. Benson concluded.

Janie cleared her throat. "How do you know Harriet killed her?"

I glanced at Matt. "What are you comfortable sharing?"

Matt let out a reluctant sigh. "All I'm willing to say at this point is that physical evidence at the scene indicates the presence of a second individual."

Gabby barked triumphantly. "You found Harriet's DNA!"

"No comment," he said in a way that nevertheless suggested Gabby was right.

"How and when did she do it?" Hialeah asked.

I cleared my throat. "Harriet persuaded Polly to accompany her to the studio apartment sometime late Friday night or early Saturday morning. Once there, she killed her."

"Why did Polly go with her?" Hialeah asked.

I shrugged. "We may never know exactly what Harriet said or did to lure Polly there. What's clear is that Harriet killed her in the studio apartment and hid the body in the professor's steamer trunk."

"What was the murder weapon?" Gabby asked.

"The same poison she used to kill the professor."

Gabby scowled. "So on Friday night, when she offed her, I was sound asleep next door?"

"Sadly, yes. You and Mr. Benson and I were almost certainly in the building when the crime occurred."

There was a moment's silence as we absorbed the fact that once again, our building had been the site of violent death.

Hialeah raised her hand. "Why did she put Polly's body in the steamer trunk?"

Janie shuddered. "I was wondering the same. Why go to all that trouble?"

"It seems so cold-blooded," Mom added. "So *diabolical*."

"Agreed," I replied. "But here's the thing: Hiding the body in the trunk was actually rather ingenious. Polly had an appointment at the sheriff's station on Saturday afternoon to sign her statement. When she didn't show, Matt and his team had to wonder if she'd made a run for it."

Matt said, "We did wonder that, yes."

"Remember — Matt and the forensic team had already searched the steamer trunk. With so much else going on, it's unlikely the trunk would have been examined again anytime soon."

"What you're saying," Mom said, "is Harriet realized the trunk would be the perfect place to hide Polly's body."

"Right."

"So if you hadn't noticed the trunk was heavier when you were helping Deputy Martinez lug it downstairs…."

"Then it would have been taken directly to the evidence shed behind the sheriff's station."

Matt spoke up. "In all likelihood, it would have been days before we found the body."

Mr. Benson shook his head. "It saddens me that Harriet — an accomplished, impressive individual — did that to Polly. The two of them were friends. They'd known each other for years."

"About that," Janie said. "I get the *who* and the *how* and the *when* of all this, but I'm still not clear *why* Harriet killed Polly and Professor Greeley. At the awards ceremony, you hinted that Greeley was blackmailing Harriet. Is that what this was about?"

My stomach tightened as I prepared my answer. Janie's question cut right to the heart of everything that had happened over the past six days.

"Well," I said, hoping the lie about to leap from my lips landed the way I wanted it to. "That's the real question, isn't it? Why did she decide to kill them? Let's start with the professor. We know he was an unpleasant, rude, angry individual — but I'm sure we all agree that obnoxiousness alone isn't sufficient motive for murder."

"Speak for yourself," Gabby muttered.

"And yes, this afternoon at the awards ceremony, I hinted that Harriet was being blackmailed by the professor." I glanced at Matt as if seeking his permission. "But actually, the opposite was true: The professor was being blackmailed by Harriet."

The room gasped.

"A few years ago, it turns out the professor did some bad, illegal things — financial things, if I understand correctly — that Harriet found out about."

"Oh, my," Mom said.

"How dreadful," Mr. Benson added.

"What bad things?" Gabby demanded. "What did he do?"

At that point, Matt jumped in as planned. "Sarah, stop. You've shared too much."

"But they deserve to —"

"Sorry, no. The details need to wait for the trial."

I frowned in a way that I hoped conveyed a mixture of frustrated disagreement and reluctant acquiescence, even though what I really felt was relief, since the financial shenanigans hadn't actually happened and we hadn't had time to invent any details.

"Okay, fine," I said with what I hoped was a suitably grumpy tone.

"If Harriet was blackmailing him," Janie said, "why would she kill him?"

I glanced again at Matt before continuing. "When Matt talked to the New Orleans police about the professor, he found out the professor called them last week and asked to meet with them when he returned to New Orleans. He told them his good name was being besmirched by a vicious criminal and demanded the miscreant be brought to justice."

Gabby exclaimed, "She was bleeding him dry and he got sick of it. So before he could turn her in, she shut him up — permanently!"

I shrugged. "Given everything that's happened, that explanation makes a lot of sense."

"Wow," Janie said, shaking her head. "What a story. How does Polly fit in?"

"Unfortunately, I think Polly knew too much. One thing I keep coming back to is a conversation that Harriet, Polly, Mr. Benson, and I had in the main tent on Friday."

Mr. Benson gave me a puzzled look. "That conversation? Why?"

"When I told them the professor's eyes were blood-red, Polly became alarmed. I think she realized what that might mean."

"You mean, she might have guessed what the poison was?"

I looked at Matt. "The state lab still hasn't identified it, right?"

He shook his head. "They know it's plant-based, but it isn't one they're familiar with. Whatever it is, it's rare."

"I'm willing to bet Polly the plant expert had a good idea what the poison was, and also knew that Harriet knew."

"And because of that," Hialeah said, "Harriet decided to kill her?"

"Sadly, yes."

Mr. Benson sat up as if realizing something. "About Harriet's confession. She might have done it to protect someone."

"Who?" Janie asked.

Mr. Benson opened his mouth but shut it

abruptly when he realized his mistake. He'd almost said *like that man who gave me Emily's letter* before remembering that Emily's letter was supposed to be a secret.

"You're saying," I said, jumping in, "that her confession might be a way to protect someone she might have been working with?"

"Yes, Sarah."

"That's certainly possible," I said, trying to sound like I was open to the possibility but not convinced.

Hialeah said, "Sarah, I appreciate you and Sheriff Forsyth sharing this information with us."

"You can thank Matt. He felt you had a right to know."

Matt looked at each of them in turn. "I hope all of you will keep this to yourselves?"

"Of course," they all lied immediately.

"Good." He stood up. "I have to get back to the station."

Following his lead, the others began gathering plates and glasses to take into the kitchen.

I walked Matt to the door. "Another long night?" I asked.

"Unfortunately." He paused at the door, his gaze tired but attentive.

I glanced behind to make sure we were out of range of prying ears. "So … about what we need to talk about."

He nodded. "Are you and Janie opening the cafe tomorrow?"

Oh, gosh — I hadn't given tomorrow even a second's thought. "I think so. Probably? Maybe a bit later than usual?"

"How about I swing by at closing. Late afternoon?"

"Sure."

His hand cupped my cheek. "See you tomorrow."

And then he was gone.

I blinked back an unexpected rush of emotion — feelings can be so pesky sometimes — and headed into the kitchen, where everyone had decided it was necessary to help clean up.

"Stop, everyone. It's just a few dishes. Shoo."

After batting away the obligatory protests, I herded them back into the living room.

"So," I said as they prepared to leave. "Are we all good here?"

I held my breath, waiting to see if they'd bought what I was selling.

"Of course," Janie said immediately.

"I appreciate everything you've done," Mr. Benson said.

"Darn tootin'," Gabby added.

Hialeah nodded. "Thank you for everything, Sarah."

At the door, Janie said, "About tomorrow...."

"Is it okay if we open a bit later? At ten?"

She smiled, relieved. "Exactly what I was thinking. See you in the morning."

And with that they headed downstairs, leaving just me, Claire, and Mom.

"Good job, girls," Mom said as she shrugged into her coat.

"Think they bought it?" I asked.

"Oh, they're going to have a lot of fun telling everyone about what they heard tonight."

Claire smiled. "That's the secret sauce, isn't it."

"Secret sauce?" Mom said.

"Lies are better — more powerful — when they're exciting and dramatic."

I sighed, relieved that the day was finally winding to close. "You two sure you don't want to stay a bit?"

Mom considered my question a few seconds before answering. "I'd love to, dear, but I am beat. I'm crawling into bed the second I get home." She pulled me in for a hug. "Let's talk tomorrow."

"I need to head out, too," Claire said.

"To parts unknown?"

"To parts you don't need to know about." She gave me a quick hug. "Thanks again for everything."

"See you soon?"

"Count on it."

CHAPTER 33

I awoke the next morning knowing exactly what I needed to do next: I needed to talk to Mom. The feeling of having left something unresolved with her had been tugging away at me, and a good night's sleep had helped me figure out what it was.

I glanced at the bedside clock — it was a few minutes before eight, which meant I had time — so I texted Mom and told her I was coming over. After a record-fast shower, I drove to her house.

In the front yard was the latest edition of the *Gazette*, its plastic wrap glistening with morning dew. I quickly skimmed the top story — "Flower Show Judge Arrested" — and smiled when I didn't see anything too objectionable.

Paper tucked under my arm, I let myself in. "Mom, you up?"

"In here," she called from the kitchen.

I found her in her bathrobe and slippers, mug in hand, waiting for the coffee to finish brewing.

I'll be honest — she looked exhausted. A week of murder and mayhem had run her down. Her shoulders were slumped, the worry lines in her forehead prominent. In her hazel eyes I saw wariness, like she was steeling herself for whatever bad news might be coming next.

As the coffee machine finished dripping, she gestured to the kitchen table. "Have a seat. Coffee's ready. Want some?"

I set the paper on the kitchen counter and took a seat. "I'm good, thanks. Were you able to sleep last night?"

"I should have, given how tired I am," she said as she poured herself a cup. "But no, not really. A lot of tossing and turning."

"Things on your mind?"

She added a healthy dollop of cream, then looked right at me. "You could say that."

It didn't take a mind-reader to know what — or rather who — she had on her mind. "I'm really sorry."

"Are you now?" she said as she joined me at the table. "For what?"

Her careful tone induced a jolt of guilt. "For not telling you the real deal yesterday. With Wendy hovering, I couldn't find a way to loop you in."

She sighed. "I'm used to that from you, Sarah. You've always been a secret-keeper."

Before I lost my nerve, I pressed forward. "Well, there's more. I'm sorry about the other reason I didn't tell you."

Her gaze sharpened. "Yes?"

"I was worried you'd try to stop me."

She nodded. "You doubted my ability to keep my emotions in check, to be part of a team, to support the team's goals. You doubted my ability to *not* mess up a plan."

More guilt rushed in. Her words, spoken calmly and simply, were precisely right. "I shouldn't have doubted you for any of that. Not even for an instant. I'm so sorry."

She reached out and clasped my hand. "I will always support you, dear. Always."

"Thank you." A wave of emotion rose within me. "I promise I won't forget that again. I know my involvement in this spy stuff bothers you, and I'm sorry for that as well. Causing you worry is the last thing I want."

She took a sip of her coffee. "I wish you weren't involved, but I don't see a way around it, not with all that's going on around here. Besides, maybe it's wrong to keep you away. Up there onstage yesterday, confronting that awful woman, you really — and there's no other word for it — *blossomed*. You were in your element. You loved every minute of it."

"Not at first. At first I thought I was going to throw up."

"What matters is you pushed through your jitters and delivered. That's your superpower, Sarah — your ability to force change. You proved that again yesterday."

I took a deep breath. "And now you're wondering if my aptitude for catching killers means I want to join Claire and Emily in Spy Land."

"Do you?"

I blinked at the suddenness of her question. "I…. Well, what I think is…."

"Take your time, dear. I know the answer isn't easy." In her tone there was sadness, like she believed she knew the answer and hated it but was determined to support me anyway. It was only then that I fully understood her subdued mood.

"Okay." I sat up straighter. "You're right. The answer isn't easy. Part of me loves doing what Claire and Emily do. Figuring stuff out. Taking down the bad guys. Beating them at their own game. All of that is thrilling and satisfying."

"Go on…."

"But what I love even more is being back in Eagle Cove." As the words left my mouth, I felt myself flushing — with *relief.* Happiness surged through me as I realized I was speaking my actual truth.

"The world I want to be part of is *here*. With

you. With … *everyone* here. I've gone through so much in the past few years. I'm ready to become the person I've always wanted to be. I know that's a cliche, but it's how I feel. I mean, look how much I've changed since returning to Eagle Cove. I'm running a cafe — me, a small business owner — and reconnecting with friends and family, and hopefully building a future with…."

A smile came to Mom's lips. "Have you made things right with him yet?"

"I'm seeing him later. Fingers crossed."

"About the person you want to be. Tell me about her."

"She's a woman who sees her mom every day —"

"Excellent — I like this woman already."

"And runs a cafe with her childhood friend and is doing pretty well with it, all things considered. And she's dating the guy she made the mistake of letting go too many years ago — the guy who hopefully still wants to date her even after she kept something really important from him."

Mom reached over and clasped my hand. "Are you sure about this? I suspect Emily and Claire would take you on if you asked."

I shook my head. "What I want is here."

For the first time in weeks, I saw her shoulders relax. "Are you hungry? Do you want breakfast?"

"I'm good. Actually, scratch that. A latte sounds great. But I'll tell you what I really want."

"What's that?"

"I want an inner circle — with you in it. I want us to be able to discuss everything and trust each other completely. No holding back."

Her eyes grew bright with emotion. "I want the same, dear."

"When it comes to the spy stuff, the people in the circle are you, me, and Matt. Plus Emily and Claire, of course. No more secrets among the five of us."

"Agreed."

"So in that spirit, I need to bring you up to speed."

Mom glanced at her half-empty mug. "Good, because I have questions. I need a refill. You said you want…?"

"A latte would be perfect."

She bustled over to the counter, the bounce in her step restored.

I rubbed my hands together as if preparing for a presentation, which is basically what I was doing. "You already know the public version of events — the stuff that came out yesterday at the flower show and in this morning's edition of the *Gazette*."

"I haven't seen the morning paper yet."

"It's on the counter. It's not a bad writeup. Nothing egregiously wrong."

"Good. Go on."

"You also know the Eagle Cove gossip version of events we shared last night with the gang."

"The version we want the town to believe is the real story."

"Right. So now, here's the inner-circle, super-secret spy version — what's really going on beneath the surface."

She returned to the table, mugs in hand.

I took hold of mine, the heat feeling lovely against my fingers. "I'll start with the background, which I'm not completely clear about, mainly because Claire and Emily are so stingy about what they share."

Mom brought her mug to her lips to hide her smile.

I knew why she was smiling — *the irony of me, Sarah Boone, complaining about someone else keeping secrets.* "We know H.U.S.H. is freaking out about something that happened decades ago. An event, weapon, device, person, organization, conspiracy — I'm not sure what — that recently resurfaced. Let's call it the Big Bad Secret."

"It's why they reactivated Emily. And the reason for all that hubbub a few months ago when they pulled those metal boxes from the lake."

"Right. But the metal boxes are only part of the puzzle. There's something else here in Eagle Cove."

"Something else?"

"It's why the spies keep coming. They're looking for something."

"For what?"

"Claire basically admitted it's information stored on a flash drive."

"What kind of information?"

"No idea, which is kind of driving me batty. The only thing I know for sure is everybody wants it."

"So that's the background."

"Right. Now, let's talk about the flower show." I brought the latte to my lips and inhaled the lovely aroma. "Over in Spy Land, H.U.S.H. learned something about the Big Bad Secret and sent a bunch of agents here."

"A bunch?"

"Claire, of course. Also Edgar."

Mom blinked. "Edgar? That nice man? The event videographer? You're saying he's…?"

"He's a H.U.S.H. agent like Claire. He's also the brother of Claire's ex-husband Ben."

"Oh, dear, that's complicated." Her brow furrowed. "I'm trying to remember — was Edgar at Claire's wedding?"

I tried to recall — fifteen years had passed since her wedding. "I don't think so."

"Why didn't he attend his brother's wedding?"

"Maybe he was on a mission for H.U.S.H.?"

Mom sighed. "I hope there isn't a rift between

the two brothers." Without warning, she bolted upright. "Wait. If Claire's a spy and Edgar's a spy, does that mean Ben's a spy, too?"

"Yep."

"And they all still work together?"

"Yep."

"Quite the tangled web."

"Claire seems fine with it, so...."

"I met Ben a few times. At the wedding, of course. Also when Claire was up here visiting her parents. I liked him. He and Claire seemed good for each other. I was sad when they divorced."

"I liked him, too. By the way, that's your superpower."

She blinked. "My superpower?"

"The way you care about the people you're close to. Nobody does it better."

"That's nice of you to say," she said, pleased. "But let's focus. You were telling me about the army of H.U.S.H. agents who descended on the flower show."

"Right. H.U.S.H. also reactivated Professor Greeley."

Mom gasped. "*Him?*"

"He used to be an agent."

"That miserable complainer was a *spy?*" She flushed. "Sorry to speak ill of the dead, but...."

"Nothing to be sorry about. He was awful. Horrid."

"Why was he here?"

"Well, that brings us to the tricky part of this." I took a second to organize my thoughts. "I think there's a divide, a schism, within H.U.S.H."

"And you believe that because…?"

"Claire brought the professor to Eagle Cove secretly, without going through the normal channels."

"Why would she do that? Oh, I see. Because she doesn't know who in H.U.S.H. she can trust?"

"Just my speculation — Claire didn't confirm squat. But I believe she trusts some people and doesn't trust others. The trust list includes Emily, Edgar, and Ben."

"Okay. So what was Professor Greeley here for?"

"To identify people involved in whatever happened decades ago."

"Did Claire tell you that?"

"Not exactly." I shared what Hialeah had told me about the professor grilling her a few hours before his death.

"Oh, my," Mom said. "The poor dear. I hope he wasn't too hard on her."

"He was asking her about longtime Eagle Cove residents. I'm guessing they were all here when the Big Bad Secret happened."

"And you think he was murdered because…?"

"Because he recognized Harriet."

"That was one of my questions. I'm assuming Harriet was also part of H.U.S.H.?"

"It turns out 'Harriet Vale' is a false identity used by a H.U.S.H. agent who was believed killed in the line of duty decades ago."

Mom shook her head. "How did she manage to fake her death and establish a new identity?"

"No idea. But plastic surgery is part of it. Claire showed me an old photograph. Harriet looks very different now."

"You weren't exaggerating when you said Eagle Cove was overrun with spies. Claire, Edgar, Professor Greeley, Harriet...."

"Plus Polly, of course. Retired, but still."

"Yes, the poor woman. I have questions about her. But first, how did Professor Greeley recognize Harriet?"

"We may never know exactly. It may have been something subtle, something behavioral — a gesture, a turn of phrase, the way she walked. Something ingrained and unconscious."

"Something she did without being aware of it."

"Whatever it was, it triggered the professor's memories. He figured out who she was. When Harriet realized that, she acted swiftly and ruthlessly."

Mom shuddered. "And nearly got away with it."

I sighed in agreement. "You know, I happened to overhear a conversation between Claire and the professor the day after he arrived. Claire was really laying into him."

"About what?"

"About being a jerk. About spending his time complaining instead of listening and learning."

"Well," she sighed, "he certainly excelled at complaining. Though in fairness to the man, it seems in the end he stepped up and did his job."

"In the end, yes, he did. And paid the ultimate price."

The two of us remained quiet for a moment in slightly reluctant tribute.

After another sip of her coffee, Mom said, "Now, about Polly. Why did Harriet have to kill her?"

"Reason One: Harriet needed a scapegoat for the professor's murder. She wrote the fake Emily letter to pin the blame on Polly."

"But couldn't she have left Polly alive? Why kill her?"

"Reason Two: It's likely Polly knew who Harriet really was."

"You say that because…?"

"They were at H.U.S.H. at the same time. They were both horticulturists. They both worked the flower-show circuit as event judges. Given all that…."

"Yes, that makes sense. And because Polly knew who Harriet used to be…."

"She had to be silenced."

Mom frowned. "If what you're saying is correct — and it certainly sounds right to me — then why did Harriet agree to come to Eagle Cove? She was free and clear of her past. She had to know H.U.S.H. is nearby. Why take the risk?"

I shrugged. "Maybe the reemergence of the Big Bad Secret put her in danger. Maybe she believed she had no choice but to come here to find the missing information."

Mom let out a sigh. "There's so much we don't know. I mean, do we know anything about the man who gave the fake Emily letter to Mr. Benson?"

"Nothing definite, but my guess is he's Harriet's son."

"Her *son*?"

"Claire told me she has a son who fits the age and description of the man who gave Mr. Benson the fake Emily letter. On stage yesterday, I hinted to Harriet that I knew he was involved. I'm pretty sure she chose to confess at least in part to protect him."

"How involved do you think he was?"

"We know he gave Mr. Benson the letter. He's most likely the person who searched our apartments on Friday afternoon. Harriet was at the flower show when that happened, so the break-in couldn't have been done by her. Also, I wouldn't be surprised if he helped his mother with the murders."

"I assume Claire's tracking him down?"

"Yes. Matt, too."

"Well, hopefully he won't get far. What about Harriet? Won't the feds or H.U.S.H. be swooping in to claim jurisdiction over her?"

"We'll see," I said with a shrug. "Harriet seems determined to avoid that. Her confession was strategic — she chose to surrender to Matt. And her attorney is apparently top-notch."

Mom shook her head. "I don't like Eagle Cove getting pulled into this spy business. These secret agents playing their games in our little town need to go someplace else. I mean, isn't that what glamorous world capitals are for?"

"Agree," I said fervently, then raised my mug. "Here's to a peaceful, happy future for Eagle Cove, free of espionage madness."

Mom clinked her mug on mine. "Amen."

CHAPTER 34

Later that afternoon, after a busy day of serving muffins and coffees to a reassuringly large throng of eager customers, Janie and I looked at each other and breathed a collective sigh of relief. Despite the utter catastrophe of our catering debut and our long weekend of nonstop bad press and — oh, yes — a double dose of violent death, folks were still flocking to Emily's Eats for lattes and treats.

The gossip helped, of course. From her strategic perch in her favorite red booth, Gabby efficiently dispensed a steady stream of "here's what really happened" to all who would listen, with Mr. Benson chipping in from his stool with clarifying details. At her table near the front window, Hialeah held session after session with clients, many of whom were curious about more than just the spirit world.

"You know, we might survive this," Janie said as the afternoon wound down and the cafe finally began emptying out.

"We might."

"I was expecting folks to keep their distance after what happened."

"I worried about the same. And who knows what's coming next? But today was a good day."

Janie glanced at her watch. "I need to finish cleaning up before heading home. Ed's shift" — her husband was a fireman with irregular hours — "starts at six."

"You go," I said. "I'll handle the cleanup."

"No, I —"

"Nope, I insist."

She gave me a grateful smile. "You sure?"

"Absolutely."

"Thank you. See you in the morning!"

A short while later, after the last customer of the day had come and gone, I flipped the cafe door's "Open" sign to "Closed" and began cleaning up.

I was wiping down a booth when I heard a knock and looked over to see Matt.

My heart thumped. The time had come for what my brain had already labeled The Big Discussion. I hustled over and let him in.

"Thank you," he said politely as he stepped inside.

"Thank you for coming," I replied, equally politely.

His gaze was calm and focused, his even-keeled temperament back in place.

"You slept," I said.

"Four wonderful hours."

"Anything new happen I need to know about?"

He shook his head. "We're wrapping things up. Just in time, too. The boys get back from Boston in a bit. I'm picking them up at the train station in" — he glanced at his watch — "ninety minutes."

"They chose the right weekend to visit their mom."

"Or the wrong one, from their perspective," he said wryly. "The mass poisoning was big news in Boston. They're insanely curious about what went down and kicking themselves for not being here. I've never gotten more texts from them."

I smiled as my thoughts went to my daughter Anna, who deserved an update. "Well, I can't blame them for being curious. What happened was crazy."

"The way you managed to wrap it up yesterday into a neat and tidy bow — that was impressive. Tap-dancing through a minefield."

I shrugged, pleased. "I didn't like having to tell all those whoppers, but when it comes to protecting the people I care about…."

"Speaking of whoppers. Last night with your gang. You think they bought it?"

"I think so. They spent the whole day blabbing everything to everyone who would listen."

"I sense a 'but.'"

"Well," I said with a sigh, "I'm pretty sure Mr. Benson told Gabby that Emily is alive and back in the spy game. And I'm pretty sure the two of them have decided to keep that juicy secret from you and me."

A smile came to his lips. "Secrets, secrets, secrets."

"Secrets complicate everything." I took a deep breath and steeled myself — it was time to tackle the elephant in the room. "I am so sorry I lied to you about Emily. I should have brought you into the loop right away."

"I appreciate you saying that," he replied, his tone steady. Clearly, he was done being upset with me. "Also, I get that the secret wasn't yours alone."

"Well," I said, pushing back a wave of anxiety. "That's not all."

"Not all?"

"Emily isn't the only person I've been holding back about."

He gazed at me silently, waiting for me to continue.

"I've been holding back about — *me*."

His brow furrowed. "Holding back how?"

"Well," I said, hoping the words came out right. "For a couple of years now, I've been afraid to take a hard look at my divorce and how it affected me. I've wanted — needed — to keep it at arm's length. I dove into a million different things to stay busy to hold my anger and sadness at bay."

He nodded. "Totally understandable. Totally normal."

"I agree. And I want to be clear: I don't regret doing that. It's what I needed to do. The emotional distance helped me. It was important for me. It *worked*."

He stayed silent, waiting for me to continue.

"But here's the thing. I'm starting to realize I don't need the emotional buffer the way I once did. It's becoming more of a hindrance than a help. Plus, I'm seeing how it affects the people I care about, including you."

At my mention of him, he went still.

"It's keeping me from opening myself up to new possibilities. From learning to trust again."

He flushed as my words sank in.

"I want to feel that trust again. I'm ready for it. Especially now." Tears filled my eyes. "With you."

He was about to swoop me into his arms — he was moving closer, his expression intent — but I shook my head. "There's more I want to say."

"I'm listening," he said, easing back, his voice husky with emotion.

"I don't regret my marriage to Ethan." Blinking back tears, I pushed on. "I have my daughter because of him. We had many good years. I was happy with him. Until I wasn't."

He remained still, giving me the space to continue.

"What I regret is letting you go all those years ago, back when I was young and foolish and oh-so-certain about everything. I look back now and think — what an idiot I was." I wiped tears away. "I know I'm not making sense. How can I regret breaking up with you but not regret marrying Ethan, which happened only because I broke up with you? I can't have it both ways. I know that. I get that. But I —"

"Hey hey hey," he said gently. "It's okay. I get what you're saying. Totally. Completely."

Through my tears, I peered up at him gratefully. Of course he understood. As a divorced dad with two teenaged sons, he'd been through much the same thing.

I took a deep breath. "I want you to know — I trust you. Fully and completely. In every possible way."

He waited for me to continue.

"I also know that trust is earned." More tears threatened but I pushed them back. "So here's my promise to you: I'm going to work my you-know-what off to earn your trust."

He blinked back a surge of emotion. "Thank you. I appreciate you saying that. I have faith you will do that. Now, can I ask you a question?"

"Yes."

"Can I please kiss you now?"

I laughed. "Yes."

He pulled me in and laid one on me and *yes oh yes oh yes* it was good. His strong arms around me felt oh so right as we lost ourselves in each other, falling deeper and deeper into the moment.

When he finally broke away, I could only stare in wonder into his gorgeous brown eyes.

"You know," he murmured, "I may on occasion have said you are the most challenging woman I've ever known."

"You have. I'm sorry about that."

"I may also have said you're the most amazing, exciting, incredible woman I've ever known."

I blinked back tears as I looked up at him.

"I want all of you, Sarah Boone. Every single part of you. Because *all* of you is what makes you *you*."

"Even the annoying parts?"

He chuckled. "I walked right into that one, didn't I?"

"You most certainly did."

"The answer is yes. Even the parts of you that I find rather, um, *challenging*."

"Thank you," I said. 'Thank you thank you *thank you*."

He brushed a strand of hair from my cheek.

"This weekend won't be our last fight. You realize that, right?"

"I do."

"We're gonna mess up. Both of us. It's gonna happen."

"I know."

"So here's my promise to you: When we mess up, we'll work through it. We'll find our way forward. Together."

Together. I blinked back tears. "I love you, Matt Forsyth."

"I love you, Sarah Boone."

I gazed up at him, scarcely able to believe my luck. "Kiss me again, you big hunka-hunka."

With a growl of anticipation, he pulled me in and murmured, "Yes, ma'am."

CHAPTER 35

After Matt left a short while later — reluctantly — to head to the train station in Middlemore, I finished cleaning the cafe and hustled upstairs to my apartment.

I was in my kitchen, emptying my dishwasher and humming a happy tune, when I heard a knock at the door.

"Coming!" I yelled, wondering who it might be. Perhaps my handsome *boyfriend* had forgotten something? Perhaps he wanted another kiss?

I opened the door and gasped aloud.

Matt wasn't there. Instead I found myself staring at —

The man I'd seen the day before. At the awards ceremony. Standing next to Claire.

The Acting Boss of H.U.S.H.

He Who We Didn't Like!

"Ms. Boone," he said.

"I know you," I blurted out.

He went still, his grey eyes alive with calculation. "Is that so?"

He looked so tall and trim in his dark suit. So sleek and forbidding with his hawk-like face and thick blond hair swept over his head. Standing before me, he gave off the vibe of — it's hard to describe — a powerful medieval lord who's up to no good.

"I mean," I stammered, "I saw you yesterday at the show. Standing at the back with Claire."

"My name is Thaddeus Graveston."

Such a weird name. Yes, that was the first ridiculous, pointless, meaningless thought that tumbled from my poor flummoxed brain.

"Mr. Graveston," I managed to say. "How can I help you?"

He paused for a moment, as if confirming he wanted to do what he'd come here to do. Then came the words that shocked me to my core:

"The killer you know as Amy has escaped from prison."

It took me a second to absorb what he'd just said.

Then — *wham.*

My heart started pounding. My stomach knotted up. I couldn't breathe.

"Amy escaped?" I whispered.

"We believe she's headed back to Eagle Cove."

I tried to speak, tried to blink, tried to move, but no words came out. What he was saying — it couldn't be happening. It simply wasn't possible.

But it was Graveston's next words that sent my whole world spinning:

"Ms. Boone, pursuant to Emergency Authorization SB34, I hereby draft you for duty with H.U.S.H. — effective immediately."

THE END

GET A FREE STORY!

A heartwarming holiday story about a handsome veterinarian and the shy, beautiful librarian he meets on Christmas Eve....

Nick and the Snowplow is a companion to *Christmas to the Rescue!*, the first novel in the Heartsprings Valley

Winter Tale series. In *Christmas to the Rescue!*, a young librarian named Becca gets caught in a blizzard on Christmas Eve, finds shelter with a handsome veterinarian named Nick, and ends up experiencing the most surprising, adventure-filled night of her life.

Nick and the Snowplow, told from Nick's point of view, shows what happens after Nick brings Becca home at the end of their whirlwind evening.

This story is available FOR FREE when you sign up for Anne Chase's email newsletter.

Go to AnneChase.com to sign up and get your free story.

ABOUT THE AUTHOR

As Anne Chase, I write small-town Christmas romances celebrating love during the most wonderful time of the year.

As Nora Chase, I write mysteries packed with murder, mayhem, and secrets galore.

My email newsletters are great ways to find out about my upcoming books.

Christmas romance: Sign up at AnneChase.com.

Mysteries: Sign up at AuthorNoraChase.com.

Thank you for being a reader.

Made in the USA
Monee, IL
23 July 2023

39759398R00187